glamour and gumballs
SURVIVAL OF THE MATED

LOLA GLASS

one

ERIN

I DIDN'T BOTHER SAYING goodbye to my old guard as I followed my new one out of the fifth-floor apartment I'd been forced to live in for the last four years.

We weren't friends.

Never would be.

And considering my new guard was the grumpy fae I'd seen on the first two episodes of the game show, *Survival of the Mated*, I was aware that my life was about to become hell.

I'd tried to ditch my guard twice in the week since I got the letter declaring I would have to play, but no dice. He was faster than me.

My new guard, Rhett, was even bigger than my last. He was at least 6'4", with light brown skin, and loose dark curls that looked like they'd missed the last few haircuts. The messiness was kind of sexy, but I wasn't about to mention that.

When we reached the armored vehicle that would be driving me to the airport, I slammed the door shut behind me.

He blinked at me, pausing for a moment outside the vehicle. He recovered quickly though, taking his seat in the front.

I didn't say a word as he pulled out of the parking garage.

He kept glancing back at me in the mirror, though.

As he pulled out onto the road, he cleared his throat and said, "Buckle up, Erin."

"Nah. If we crash, I'm hoping it'll kill me before I have to mate with some bastard."

He blinked at me again, through the mirror.

Someone behind us honked.

He turned onto the road just long enough to pull off to the side, so he wasn't blocking anyone else. "Buckle up," he repeated.

"No."

"We're not moving until you're buckled."

"Thank fuck for that. Do you have a knife?"

"A knife?"

"So I can cut the seatbelts, and we can stay here forever."

He blinked yet again.

I draped my legs over the seat, pressing my back to the car's uncomfortable door.

"Is there a reason in particular that you want to stay here?" he finally asked.

"I think avoiding being forced to wear a bikini on television while a bunch of assholes compete to win me like a prize is reason enough," I said pleasantly.

"Ah."

"Mmhm."

A few minutes of silence went by.

I didn't budge, though my back was starting to hurt.

"What will it take to get you to buckle?" he finally asked.

"Brainwashing, probably."

He grunted.

Two more tense minutes passed.

"I can't do anything to stop the competition. There are too many fae on death's doorstep for that. They won't let you go. I can make your life easier on the island, though," he said.

My eyes narrowed. "I'm listening."

"I can call the stylists and send them out for whatever you want to wear."

That was something.

Not enough, but something.

He studied me in the mirror. "I can make them land the plane instead of forcing me to toss you out."

That was better.

He was closer.

"I'll make them pack you a small bag of toiletries, and a blanket too. With whatever you want in it. If you want anything more than that, you'll have to come out and say it."

I let out a long breath, staring out the window across from me. "I want rice given out at every challenge so I don't have to starve when the gigantic assholes refuse to ration it," I finally said.

Rhett dipped his head. "I'll make a call."

"I'll wait."

He studied me again, as if waiting for me to change my mind.

I didn't.

Rhett finally hit a few buttons on the car's console screen. I saw him tap on the name of a contact, Christina Cassette, and the phone started to ring.

"Who's Christina?" I asked.

"She and her mate lead the Society," Rhett said.

"And you have her phone number?" My voice was skeptical.

He lifted a shoulder.

Christina answered the phone. "Hey, Rhett. Is everything okay with the new Survival girl? Erin, right?"

She knew my name?

My skepticism grew.

"Yeah, she's in the car right now. She's not willing to play unless we make a few changes."

There was a moment's pause. "That's fair. The way they treated Molly wasn't acceptable. What is she hoping for?" she finally asked.

No way in hell was the woman one of the Society's leaders. She was way too *nice*.

"She wants to choose what she wears, and for the plane to land, so she can avoid skydiving. A bag of toiletries and a blanket, too. And she wants rice, given at every challenge so the contestants can't eat it all on the first day."

"All of those requests are reasonable. I had already arranged for the plane's landing, the blanket, a pillow, and a change of clothes for her. I'll call the stylists to make sure they're aware that she gets to approve her wardrobe, and that they're to go out and get whatever she wants after she's seen what they chose. They can grab the toiletries while they're out. The rice will take convincing, but I'll make it happen."

"What proof do I have that you are who Rhett says you are?"

I countered. She probably didn't know she was on speaker, but her surprise didn't matter.

I was the one who was about to be dropped on a tropical island with a dozen horny fae assholes.

"Hi, Erin." Christina's voice remained pleasant. "I suppose I don't have any proof to give you over the phone, but I lead the Society alongside my mate, Charlie. Our son, Cameron, won Survival's first season. Given that the first contestant, Molly, is our new daughter-in-law, it's in our best interest to make sure the second season runs more smoothly for you. I'd have a hard time convincing her that I'm sorry for the shit she went through if I didn't change anything for you, don't you think?"

My forehead creased.

That made sense, but it wasn't proof.

"If the stylists don't let you choose what to wear and provide you with what you need, then you can simply refuse to get on the plane. If they do, you'll know I'm in enough of a position of power to make that happen, correct?"

"I guess." My voice was reluctant.

"There will have to be some level of trust involved to have the rice delivered consistently. Even if there wasn't, I think we both know that Rhett could get you there by force if he wanted. Keeping the peace rather than muscling their way through everything is a choice fae males make. I was human once, too. I understand the difference in strength better than most."

She was?

My defenses eased slightly.

"Alright, fine. I'm not cooperating if the stylists aren't aware of the change in plans when I get there, though," I said.

"That's perfectly fair. You'll find them ready and waiting. Good luck, Erin. I hope this experience ends up far better than you're expecting."

The call ended, and I felt Rhett's eyes on me in the mirror once more.

Had he been staring at me the whole time?

I wasn't sure how to feel about that.

"Buckle up," he said again.

"I don't know why you're so concerned with my safety." I finally removed my legs from the bench seat and turned to sit properly.

"It's my job." He pulled onto the road again as soon as I was buckled.

"We're in an armored vehicle, and everyone loves the fae. It's not like I'm in any danger."

He grunted, and said nothing else.

I glared out the window through the rest of the ride.

AS CHRISTINA PROMISED, the stylists were ready and waiting for the wardrobe change. They told me how many clothing items I was allowed to bring, and had me list out exactly what I wanted, down to brands I liked.

Two of them disappeared immediately to get that stuff, and everything else Christina had asked for.

As much as I didn't want to admit it, there was some evidence that she was who she said she was. Rhett hadn't called anyone else before we arrived, and someone had spoken with the team before we got there.

I refused most of the processes the stylists had planned. I wasn't wearing eyelash extensions, or getting highlights, or anything else that would change what I looked like. My body was mine; if the fae only wanted me with a makeover, they could find someone else.

Because of my refusals, we were done early. So, I spent two hours sitting on a couch, eating way too many of the pastries that had been provided by the Society. Rhett had confiscated my phone the moment I pulled it out of my pocket, so there was nothing else to do.

When the stylists returned, I put on the sports bra, shorts, and long-sleeved tee I'd requested, all in black.

Then, I went through the bag of items I'd been promised. When I was satisfied everything was there, I followed Rhett out of the building and got on the plane like a good little compatible mate.

My throat constricted as we took off, heading straight for my personal hell.

• • •

I MANAGED a few hours of sleep through the eleven-hour flight, though they were all restless. I tried to watch a few movies, but mostly ended up staring out the window while fighting off feelings of panic.

I was trapped.

So very trapped.

And every time I glanced at Rhett, I found him looking at me.

I didn't bring that up. Or question it.

There was too much other shit to consider.

There was another guy just as big as Rhett on the plane too, but Rhett didn't chat with him. I didn't recognize him from the first season of Survival, so I had no idea who he was.

WHEN WE FINALLY LANDED, I was ready to get out of the flying hunk of metal and get the game show over with.

If only I had bargained to make the contest three days, instead of thirty.

The chance of Christina agreeing to that seemed near zero, but still. I should've *tried*.

I unbuckled my seatbelt and stood up, stretching my back a little as Rhett picked up the hiking backpack that had been stuffed full of my new things.

When he held the straps out, I slipped my arms through them. He reached out to buckle the bits that would hold it in place around my chest and waist, but I swatted his hand away and buckled it myself.

"You're protecting me, right?" I asked him.

"Yes," he confirmed, at the same time the other man in the plane stepped up beside him and said, "No."

I blinked at them both.

Rhett's forehead creased as he looked at the other guy.

"Christina sent me with this." He handed over a thick envelope with Rhett's name written in cursive on the front.

Rhett ripped the envelope open and pulled out a card. Murder filled his eyes as he read it. Strangely, I felt safe enough with the guy not to feel the need to step away from him.

"I'm Jordan," the newcomer said. "I'll be your guard on the island while Rhett competes with the other men."

"Like fuck I will," Rhett snarled.

My eyebrows shot upward. "He's in the game?"

"No," Rhett said, at the same time the other guy said, "Yes."

I snagged the card from Rhett's hand and read it myself.

You're the twelfth man competing on the island. Jordan is taking your place as the guard.

The Society needs you. We need you. Don't let yourself fade.

Love,

Christina

P.S. We both know that if your mother was still here, she would've forced you into every game that's happened. Play this one for her.

My eyebrows lifted higher.

Rhett took the card back and crumpled it. "I'm not fucking doing it. You can compete, or you can fly back when this plane leaves," he told Jordan flatly.

Jordan snorted. "Everyone is aware that I'm only interested in men. There would be bloodshed if the Society sent me to play for a woman. Too many bastards wanted the chance to be here. You have to play, if just to keep the peace."

"Just tell them to vote you out first," I told Rhett.

Rhett leveled me with his glare. "Every male on the island knows I don't want a mate."

"But they also know you're straight," Jordan said. "There's no way around playing. Stop bitching about it and get off the plane." He opened the door and hit a button to lower a set of stairs, then put a hand on my lower back and started propelling me out.

The hand was ripped away almost as soon as it touched me.

"Don't touch her. Do you want one of these bastards to kill you?" Rhett snarled.

I remembered seeing Rhett steady Molly with a hand on her arm in the first season. It couldn't have been against the rules.

So why was he getting angry at Jordan for it?

"Alright, I'm going," I tossed back, stepping out onto the stairs.

I made it to the bottom of them before I realized it was raining outside.

Shit.

When I tried to turn around, I found a massive, glowering Rhett behind me, blocking the path.

Jordan was behind him.

I wasn't getting back on the plane.

All of my stuff was going to get wet.

The blanket and the spare clothes I had bargained for?

They would be useless, at least until the rain stopped.

"Keep going. The other guys will be arriving soon," Jordan said. "Rhett, you should take to the sky and fly down with them."

The look he gave Jordan said hell could freeze over and he still wouldn't be flying with the other men.

I looked up at the sky, pleading with it to stop raining.

Thunder rumbled overhead, promising it had no plans to do what I wanted.

Dread tightened my abdomen.

Another plane flew overhead, and the other eleven contestants jumped out. I barely glanced at them as they flew down.

"Walk this way," Jordan said.

I reluctantly shuffled a few feet in the direction he wanted me. My running shoes were already filling with sand. I had a pair of sandals in my backpack, for that reason.

At least *they* were waterproof.

All eleven of the other fae landed, most of them looking between me, Rhett, and Jordan as they tried to figure out what was going on.

At Jordan's instruction, they lined up with Rhett on the beach.

The rain was growing heavier, but the fae bastards didn't even seem to notice.

I looked over all of them, trying to forget the falling water and focus on the game I was about to be submerged in.

Other than Jordan, there was only one guy I didn't recognize from the first two episodes of the first season of Survival. I'd watched it repeatedly, trying to memorize the names, faces, and personalities so I wouldn't be starting from zero.

Silently, I went down the row.

Kyle—obnoxious, dominant asshole. Water elemental fae. Blond hair, blue eyes.

Travis—laid-back, quiet guy. Mental magic of some kind. Pale skin and dark hair.

Kaden—bronze skin, bright smile. A little too friendly. Earth elemental.

Chris—tan skin, brown hair, friendly but not awkwardly so. White feathered wings, marking him as an air elemental.

Ev—laid-back and smart. Telepath. Brown skin and curly black hair.

Julian—quiet, cunning, observational. Light skin and hair. Also a telepath.

Harker—outgoing, a little obnoxious, but quiet when necessary. Fire elemental. Golden, feathered wings.

Jim—lazy, vulgar, annoying. Blond hair, tan skin. Water elemental, so a dragon.

Reid—quiet, introverted. Dark skin and hair, and brooding eyes. Mental magic of some kind.

Colt—easygoing, quieter. Tan skin, brown hair. Mental magic of some kind.

And then there was Rhett, who also had mental magic. His glass-like wings proved it. While all the other men had colors in their wings, his were like blank slates.

The final competitor was the second guy with furry brown wings. I was pretty sure that made him an earth elemental.

Looking at all of the men told me that the winner of the last season had been Cameron, the phoenix shifter who had been working with Molly during the game after being her guard for a handful of years. On second thought, Christina had confirmed that.

The only other guy missing was Oren, and he had seemed like a creep.

"Welcome to the second season of Survival of the Mated," Jordan announced. "As you've probably realized, Rhett Rapture is joining as a competitor this season. And yes, the Society made that decision for him." He winked.

Understanding dawned in multiple men's eyes. A few of them shot him apologetic looks.

"Thanks to Oren's *departure* last season, we also welcome Ian Anders to the game. I assume our lovely leading lady knows everyone else?" he looked at me.

I dipped my head.

"Perfect." His lips stretched in a polished grin. "Now, would you like to introduce yourself?"

Jordan was still talking to me.

He nodded in encouragement, as if that was what I was looking for.

"I'm Erin," I said. "And I wanted to come here about as much as Rhett did."

One of the guys coughed back a snort.

A few lifted their eyebrows.

Three frowned.

Two grinned.

Kyle was one of the latter.

"Well," Jordan said, clearing his throat. "Let's jump into the first challenge, shall we? We're starting this season the same way we started the last, with a race through the jungle. There are two bags of necessary tools and weapons —the men who find them earn an afternoon with Erin. The last man back loses his vote in tomorrow night's council."

He counted down from three, and then the men took off into the island's jungle.

All of the men, except Rhett.

ERIN

RHETT FOLDED his arms over his chest, glowering into the jungle like it had personally harmed him.

I didn't ask why.

He was obviously hoping to get voted out ASAP.

I plopped down on my ass on the sand, slicking my damp, red hair out of my eyes. "Do you have access to the weather forecast here?" I asked Jordan.

He snorted. "No."

I sighed. "Any idea how long the rain's going to keep going?"

A loud bout of thunder rolled through.

The clouds around us were getting darker by the minute.

The rain was getting heavier, too.

"Am I allowed to snuggle with *you* in the shelter?" I asked Jordan. "All of my stuff is going to be too wet to keep me warm."

Since he wasn't playing, he seemed like the best option.

"Nope."

My grimace deepened. "Why not?"

"I don't have a death wish. The bastards here are possessive." He lifted a shoulder. "And I'm supposed to be neutral."

"Of course you are. The only person on my side in this, is me," I drawled.

He shrugged. "Your mate will be on your side when you've picked him."

As if *that* was what I wanted.

"Human women should be required to *agree* to playing this game. Most of us don't want to be a game show's prize," I said flatly.

Jordan shrugged again. "I don't have the connections to make that happen, so don't look at me."

I glared at him anyway.

All three of us waited in silence for the next few minutes, until the first guy burst through the trees. His wings were spread behind his back, the stained-glass-like surface glittering despite the lack of sunshine.

It was Reid.

I was just as uninterested in him as I was in the other guys.

He landed and smiled at me, offering a hand.

I didn't take it, or get up from my seat on the sand.

His smile started to fade.

I felt slightly bad, but ignored it.

I didn't want a mate at all. But a mate who was excited about the game, and wanted to have a cheerful conversation about our pasts or hobbies or whatever?

Not a chance.

Reid sat down a few feet from me.

Two more men were close behind him. Ian, the new guy, and Colt.

Both grinned and greeted me as they took seats beside Reid.

I answered their questions as shortly as possible.

Ian tried to keep the conversation going anyway, until Reid elbowed him in the side, silently telling him to shut up.

Friendliness had been their go-to strategy with Molly, but they were probably realizing that wasn't going to work with me.

And I hoped they'd already realized it hadn't actually worked on Molly. Considering she and Cameron had been playing everyone, and they had won, it was safe to assume no one had picked up on their plan soon enough to do something about it.

A handful more guys joined us. Some of them were bruised and bleeding, which made me think they'd tried to fight someone else for the weapons and tools.

When Kyle came jogging out of the jungle, whooping, I bit back a sigh.

The guy closest to me scooted over, as if blocking the seat from Kyle.

Kyle tossed the bag in the air, ignoring the blood dripping off his hands, arms, and chest thanks to the rain. He was a wreck, though it had obviously worked out for him.

He pointed at me, flashing a grin that could've made someone else's heart flutter.

Not mine, though even I could admit he was gorgeous.

"Get ready for the first of many dates, Erin," he declared.

I grimaced.

Yay.

TWENTY MINUTES LATER, I climbed onto a boat with Kyle and Reid. I liked Reid more than most of the other guys, though I didn't know a whole lot about any of them. Him included.

I expected both of them to try to talk to me.

Instead, after I folded myself onto the far side of the bench I was sharing with them, neither of them bothered.

They launched right into a strategy discussion.

"You're a threat now," Reid told Kyle.

Kyle snorted. "I made it to the end and *didn't win*."

"But you made it to the end," Reid pointed out. "Now, everyone knows you'll make it there again if they don't get rid of you the first chance they get. No one will expect us to team up. If we do, we can work together to change your outcome this time."

"If we work together, we're going to get to the end, and she'll pick you. The same way Molly picked Cameron."

"Not necessarily," Reid countered.

"Do you guys realize I'm sitting right here?" I interrupted.

Reid flashed me a look of apology. "We need to talk strategy before chaos breaks out on the island."

Chaos, huh?

For the first time since we landed, something made me kind of excited.

And yeah, it was the possibility of chaos.

"Sorry, Er." Kyle pronounced the attempted nickname like "*air*". "Is it okay if I call you that?"

It was better than the nickname he'd given Molly.

And he *had* actually asked if he could use it, which was far preferable than just going for it. But yeah, that wasn't happening.

"No," I said. "My name is Erin."

Kyle nodded. "No nicknames. Got it." He looked back at Reid. "The look Erin gave Jim told me she doesn't like him, and we all know Rhett will refuse if she chooses him in the end. What would be the point of working with you when I can stick with them, and increase the odds of winning?"

My eyebrows lifted.

Kyle had noticed that I didn't like Jim?

How?

When?

He hadn't seemed perceptive on the last season. Not in the episodes I'd seen, at least.

And would Rhett actually *refuse* if I chose him?

I thought about him sitting on the sand, letting go of his vote without a second thought.

Yeah, he probably *would* turn me down.

"I have Ev, Julian, and Colt" Reid said. "That's seven between our two alliances. Six tonight, without Rhett's vote, which is still a majority. We can get rid of everyone else until we're the final seven, then battle it out for the final three. Since no one expects you and your people to win, everyone will want to take you with them."

Kyle nodded slowly. "Sounds pretty simple."

"Exactly," Reid agreed.

The boat continued driving around, weaving between and around small islands while rain fell on us. It wasn't pouring, but it definitely wasn't sprinkling anymore.

Kyle and Reid continued talking strategy while I stared out at the horizon, willing the rain to stop.

It didn't.

I FELT like a popsicle when the boat finally docked at the island we would call home. It was the same island they'd used the last season, but everything they had built seemed to have been destroyed.

The men kept working on a shelter as we walked up the beach, though a few of them greeted me.

Though I'd expected Rhett to be brooding on the beach, I found him cutting bamboo with murder in his eyes.

He was obviously still unhappy about where he'd ended up.

So was I.

After a waved greeting, I told the cluster of men that I needed some air. After dropping my soaked bag, socks, and shoes at the base of a large tree, I headed down the beach.

All my things were soaked.

I was already cold, and it was still the middle of the day. That would get much worse if the rain didn't stop when the sun went down.

Considering the sky was dark as far as I could see, I didn't think it was going to let up.

Which meant I was going to have to sleep next to at least one fae, just to stay warm.

I walked down the beach until I couldn't see or hear any of the guys. The sand was soft beneath my toes, and I figured it would feel nice if it hadn't felt like I was walking on a frozen, gas station slushie.

But it did.

So, it didn't feel nice.

When I found a rock big enough to hold me, I stopped and folded myself on top of it. The rain was starting to fall harder, but I tried not to care.

I didn't succeed, but I tried.

The rock felt icy beneath me, but started warming up after a few minutes.

Shivering lightly, I stared at the ocean as the rain fell.

The only way I'd warm up was if I cuddled up with a guy.

In the middle of the day.

I'd pass.

The waves were crashing harder than they had been when our plane first landed, which told me that the wind was getting worse.

Great.

I knew some parts of the world had stormy seasons, and could only hope that what we were seeing was just a thunderstorm. Not the start of a whole month of them.

The hellish game would get much worse if it was raining constantly.

Still watching the waves, I let out a long, slow breath.

The rain falling on my skin was driving me mad, but I couldn't let myself focus on that.

I had bigger problems.

Bigger problems, like *Survival.*

My mind went back to the way Kyle and Reid hadn't included me in their conversation.

That was probably my fault. They assumed I wasn't playing, because I didn't want to be there. They might not have even realized what role Molly had played in clearing out the island with Cameron, considering they were back on the next season just a few days after the first was over. Many of the episodes likely hadn't even been edited yet.

So they didn't think I was a part of the game.

But... I was.

Wasn't I?

Why couldn't I be?

I couldn't be voted out any more than I could choose to walk away.

So, why wouldn't I play?

I bit my lip, still watching the waves crash.

As much as I'd tried to avoid the truth, there was no way out. I was on the island, and the game would end with me choosing a partner to share my life with. I didn't like knowing that, but my dislike didn't make it any less true.

And if I had to choose a partner, I needed to play the game.

But... which of the men did I want?

My forehead creased, my brows furrowing as I tried to think about all of them once again. I didn't know enough about any of them after the two episodes I'd seen to choose one. Molly had Cameron, and trusted him enough to just go with him—but I didn't have that.

Which meant I needed to get to know the bastards trying to win me over.

I sighed, loudly.

The crease between my brows smoothed.

I set my hands down on the cold, rough stone on either side of my ass and leaned back a little as I considered it.

Getting to know the guys wasn't enough to really understand whether or not I wanted to mate with them.

Anyone could pretend to be someone they weren't for a few weeks for the sake of fooling me into keeping them alive with a mate bond. I couldn't trust the answers they gave or the conversations we had.

My mind flicked back to my childhood.

My mother's asshole of a boyfriend.

The way he'd hurt both of us.

The excuses she'd given.

How normal and nice he could seem, up until he snapped.

The way she'd loved him, no matter what he did to us.

My cheeks puffed with air before I let out a shaky breath.

I couldn't put myself in that situation, game be damned. It was far too easy to be manipulated when you fell in love with someone manipulative.

But to avoid it, I needed to see the men stressed.

Angry.

Hurt.

The island's starvation would help with that, but they were big dudes, and they had magic. Their bodies could probably sustain themselves better than mine could.

So, I would have to get them to the point of stress and anger myself.

My mind went back to what Kyle and Reid had discussed.

Chaos.

They were worried about the chaos.

What if I could make that chaos happen?

Or make the existing chaos worse?

I didn't know how to push a fae guy. I really only knew what little I'd been able to talk out of my guards, when it came to them and their magic.

But I might be able to spread rumors myself if I could manage to make some of the men think I was actually befriending them. My lack of introduction at the beginning of the game made that more difficult, but I could get there.

Probably.

Maybe.

Okay, fine, making friends wasn't one of my fortes. Not even a little.

But for the sake of not ending up married to an abusive asshole, I could learn.

Hopefully.

Until then... well, I didn't like Reid much. At least Kyle had been polite and friendly when he tried to give me a nick-name. Reid had basically ignored me.

So, why not try to get him out the way I'd seen Molly get rid of Julian? I could stick with him. Focus on him. Pay attention to him.

Or I could try, at least.

I nodded at the ocean, my mind made up.

I was going to cause chaos.

Somehow.

three

ERIN

MAKING friends on the island turned out to be even harder than making friends back at home.

Every time I tried to start a conversation with a guy, he would chat pleasantly for all of one minute before finding an excuse to walk away, heading right into a group of other guys.

And I wasn't comfortable enough to talk to a whole group.

So, I went looking for someone else, until they did the same thing.

The only person I didn't try to talk to was Rhett, because he still looked murderous. As much as I disliked my situation, and didn't feel like I was in danger, I wasn't ready to be killed by a gorgeous fae dude.

My frustration grew as the day went on.

The men had obviously figured out Molly's strategy in the last season—or had at least realized that befriending her made them a target—so they were keeping things neutral with me when they weren't in a group.

Eventually, I gave up on friendship and plopped down at the base of a tree that kept me somewhat shaded from the rain. Plenty of water still leaked through its leaves, but it was better than being out in the middle of it.

I spent the rest of the day watching the guys build. They didn't seem fazed by the rain, chatting away as they built multiple shelters. They were a lot more effective than they had been in the episode I'd seen of the first season. Experience was probably to blame for that.

And they weren't building one big shelter the way they had the last time. Instead, they put together four medium ones. The medium ones seemed sturdier than the large one I'd seen on the first season, which was probably necessary considering the rain hadn't stopped.

THE WIND STARTED PICKING up around dinner time. My teeth started chattering, but no one seemed to notice. Even if they did, they'd probably rather let me suffer than risk getting close to me.

Harker was the only fire elemental on the island, so he cooked a small pot of rice for everyone to share, blocking out the storm with his wings.

Kyle eyed me when he handed me the leaf that was functioning as my bowl. I assumed he'd been elected to give it to me since everyone assumed I wouldn't choose him.

I probably wouldn't, so they weren't wrong.

"You're cold," he said.

"Nah," I said, teeth still chattering.

His forehead creased in concern, and he crouched down in front of me.

My hand shook as I lifted the leaf to my lips and bit into the sticky pile of rice. The empty pit in my stomach made it the most delicious thing in the world.

"No one wants you to suffer, Erin. We're all keeping our distances for the sake of the game, but if the weather is too much, you need to tell us."

My frustration flared. "What will you do if it is?"

"A group of us will warm you together. We'll take turns. It'll be a big snuggle-fest." He flashed me a grin.

Fuck, he was pretty.

I scoffed anyway. "I don't want a dozen assholes taking turns touching me. This isn't a petting zoo."

He chuckled. "I get it. The door's always open, though."

With that, he stood and strode away.

My frustration swelled higher.

None of the guys were willing to risk becoming a target to help me stay warm.

That probably meant I'd be sleeping alone, too, because I wasn't about to be sandwiched between *two* fae dicks.

Literally or figuratively.

Which was just grand.

I'd probably die of hypothermia on my first night playing Survival.

Yay.

MY RICE WAS GONE TOO QUICKLY, LEAVING me staring at my leaf sadly.

If only the other men had offered me their food the way they had for Molly on her season. I would've taken it without batting an eye.

Roaring laughter broke out in the group of men a ways behind me, and my head jerked backward to see what was going on before I could stop it.

There was a whole group of them. Maybe even all of them.

My gaze moved over the group, counting.

Eleven.

There were only eleven there.

Jordan was sitting in a tree somewhere, just watching me suffer.

So who was missing?

I raked my mind until the answer hit me hard.

I should've put that together immediately.

Rhett wasn't a part of the group.

Had I even seen him around recently?

I looked back out at the ocean, frowning as I considered it.

Nope, hadn't seen him.

He didn't want to be on the island at all... so maybe he would agree to keep me warm?

Tenuous excitement had me making my way to my feet. My knees knocked together as I shivered violently, and I had to catch myself on a tree, but I managed.

"Erin," Kyle called from the group. "You good?"

I looked at him long enough to give a thumbs-up, then went looking for Rhett.

The "bathroom" was empty—I called out to check, didn't risk going close.

The main strip of beach was empty.

The shelter was too.

I was all the way across the island, nearly back to the rock I'd claimed as a seat earlier, when I finally found him.

He was sprawled out on the sand, massive legs stretched

out in front of him. His shirt had been discarded, and his wings had made an appearance.

They were beautiful, and looked more masculine without the color the other men's possessed somehow.

He'd changed into a pair of basketball shorts at some point, like most of the other men were wearing. I figured they had been in one of the supply bags, since he'd been wearing cargo shorts when we first landed.

After a moment of hesitation, a heavy gust of wind blew through the trees, and I surged forward.

Nope, I wasn't walking away without at least asking about sharing body heat. Not even maybe.

I padded across the slushy-like sand, no longer feeling the chill between my numb toes. He didn't look up when I stopped next to him, though I was positive he'd noticed me.

"Hey," I said, raising my voice.

He grunted in response. I barely heard it over the wind.

"Can I sit by you?" I asked.

That didn't get me a response either.

I was too cold to wait, so I just plopped down next to him. "I'll take that as a yes," I said, scooting up closer without touching him.

The bastard basically radiated heat. I guess that was a benefit of being a massive, magical fae.

My teeth chattered loudly, and Rhett finally turned his glare toward me. "You're shivering."

"I noticed."

"Why aren't you pressed up against one of the assholes who wants a mate?"

"They don't want to risk getting voted off. Told me it was a group hug or nothing."

"And you chose nothing?"

"I'm not looking to start my own harem."

He let out a snort, and finally wrapped an arm around the back of me. When he slid me closer, removing the few inches I'd left between us, I almost moaned.

"I'm going to shamelessly use you for warmth," I mumbled as I pressed my face to his gloriously bare chest.

"Let's hope it gets me voted out."

"I'll cross my fingers for you," I agreed.

He chuckled. The sound was so soft, I wondered if I'd imagined it.

"Reid and Kyle were talking about bringing you to the end just because you'd refuse if I picked you," I said against his chest.

He grumbled. "Bastards."

"Why are they so sure?"

"I had a mate," he said.

I blinked. My eyelashes probably tickled his chest when I did.

I thought mating was permanent.

"Not a bonded mate," he said. "She wasn't compatible. Just a human."

Oh.

So he didn't *really* have a mate. He had just loved someone.

Which seemed more like a real mate to me than the loveless bond I'd end up with, but I wasn't about to say that.

"I've never been interested in repeating the experience," he said. "They're all aware of that."

Ah.

So it hadn't ended well.

Or she'd grown old and he'd taken care of her until she passed on, which sounded worse in some ways. Better in others.

"Well that works out for me," I said. "Because if it keeps raining like this, I'll need a heater every night."

He chuckled again.

It was still so quiet I almost wondered if I'd imagined it.

"I have a question, from one unwilling player in this game to another." I was still speaking against his chest, but it didn't seem to bother him.

Another strong gust of wind blew through, and I shivered a bit. One of his wings wrapped carefully around my back, blocking out all of the remaining chill. The pressure of it was surprisingly pleasant.

"Alright," Rhett said, after a few minutes. "What is it?"

"If I were to possibly want to create some chaos, how would I do it?"

There was a moment's pause.

A long moment.

"Why?" Rhett finally asked.

"Personal reasons that I'd rather not share."

After a period of silence, he said, "Pheromones."

"Pheromones?" The confusion in my voice was thick.

"Yes."

I gave him a minute before saying, "I'm going to need you to clarify. I have no idea what you mean by that."

He let out a slow breath.

Somehow, the sound and motion of it relaxed me. I leaned against him a little more, and he pulled me slightly closer.

"When a compatible mate starts looking for someone to share her bed with, she gives off pheromones. They pull willing fae in. It's basically a physical sign that you're horny."

Oh.

I bit my lip. "And that would cause chaos, how?"

"They trigger possessiveness, which grows more difficult to control as unmated fae age. All of these men are old, so they're bombs waiting to go off. Ignite the pheromones and flirt with someone, and you'll start a war they can't fight because it's in their head."

"Damn, you're vicious," I remarked.

He rewarded me with another quiet chuckle, which made my lips curve upward.

"They're being really careful about not letting me be alone with anyone," I said.

"You'll have to be clever about it, then."

My smile widened a bit more.

I was liking this plan more by the minute.

"You'll let me sleep by you, right?" I asked, a heartbeat later. "They're going to let me freeze unless I join their circus."

"Thought it was a harem."

"Same difference."

He snorted. "No."

"No, you won't let me sleep by you?"

"No, it's not the same difference." There was a pause before he said, "I'll let you share my warmth. Can't let you freeze to death in your stubbornness."

"Finally, my stubbornness gets me something I want. And something you want too, since it could make you a target."

"We can only hope."

I laughed, and his grip around my back tightened for a moment before relaxing again. I didn't ask why. Maybe I surprised him or something.

Both of us fell quiet as we watched the waves roll and crash. For the first time all day, there was no water falling in my eyes, and it was glorious. I wasn't going to move unless I had to.

"What kind of magic does everyone here have?" I asked him, after a few minutes passed. "I know all the elemental kinds, but what about the mental magic?"

Rhett let out a slow breath that had my shoulders relaxing again for some reason.

Damn, he was warm.

And strong.

But I wasn't thinking about the last part.

Not. Thinking. About. It.

"There are four kinds of mental magic. It's technically called *glamour*, though no one uses the title. There's telepathy, which is mind reading and mental speech. Julian and Ev have that. Travis has compulsion, which can push you to do something you don't want to. No one here has dream magic. Oren did, and was killed after he used it on Molly in the last season."

My eyebrows shot upward.

Hot damn.

"Illusions are the last type of magic. Myself, Reid, and Colt have that."

My eyes widened. "Illusions? Like you can make people see things that aren't there?"

"Yes." He confirmed it. "See, feel, smell, hear, and touch. All of the senses are involved."

"Holy hell. Can you use it on me? I want to see."

"Mind magic is forbidden on the island."

"Unless the contestant gives you permission," I countered.

Rhett grunted. "My illusions aren't as strong as they used to be. You won't be impressed."

"I still want to try it."

He made a noise of complaint, but a moment later, my world slowly started to spin.

I gripped him tighter.

When the spinning ended, I was sitting on the same beach we occupied, but in a vastly different situation.

The sun was shining above me, making my skin warm all over.

I had sunglasses on my face, dulling the shine of it, and I was sprawled out on a lounge chair.

There was a bar behind me serving drinks, and a refreshingly cold glass in my hand.

I could hear the waves rolling lightly, and could taste salt on my lips when there had been rain a moment earlier.

It didn't feel like *reality*, but it did feel *real*, if that made sense. I could tell it wasn't genuinely happening, but the sensations made it nice anyway.

"Damn," I breathed, watching dolphins jump out of the water as they swam past the beach.

It was beautiful.

Calm.

Peaceful.

Warm

And despite knowing it wasn't genuine, it felt good.

The image slowly faded away, and I noticed the water on my skin and in my hair once again.

The cold, too.

Rhett's warmth felt even more significant against me as the illusion disappeared.

"That was amazing," I whispered.

"And here I was, hoping you'd hate it enough to kick me off the island."

I rolled my eyes.

Rhett couldn't sell that lie. He might not have wanted to be there, but he had made the illusion nice for me. He obviously wasn't trying to make me fear him.

"If I had the power to remove anyone, I'd remove Jim," I said.

"Why Jim?"

"He made a misogynistic comment on the first episode of the last season."

Rhett grunted.

"You don't sound surprised," I said.

"I'm not."

That was all the information he was giving me on the topic, I supposed.

"So, about the pheromones," I began. "How do I start them? Do I just think about something sexy?"

"I don't know. I have no experience with pheromones."

Right.

"Did Molly's start on the island?"

"Yes. After things grew intimate between her and Cam."

Lovely.

"So I need to fuck someone?"

"Not necessarily. I think it has more to do with the emotions it causes."

I made a face. "I'll have to try masturbating to see if I can come up with some emotions, then."

Rhett made a noise that told me absolutely nothing.

Before I could ask why, he let out a short breath. "Someone's coming."

"The whole harem, probably."

His snort was impossible to ignore.

"Better make it look like you're trying to feel me up if you want to piss them off enough to get you off the island," I said.

"If I thought that would work, I'd consider it."

I didn't know why it *wouldn't* work.

Maybe because he said they all knew he didn't plan on taking a mate.

"Hey, Erin," Kyle called out. "Rhett."

I lifted a hand in a wave, barely avoiding Rhett's wing as I did. The fae seemed careful with those, so I figured I'd better dodge them when possible.

There were three other guys with Kyle, but I didn't glance their way. Doing so would mean removing my face from Rhett's blissfully warm shoulder.

"We're breaking out the desserts we found in the bags if you want some," Kyle said. "There's some kind of packaged brownies. And gumballs."

"Gumballs?" My eyebrows lifted, but I didn't lean away from Rhett's heat.

"An assload of them," Reid confirmed. "One of the supply bags was filled to the brim with gum."

Well, that was a waste of space.

But thinking about gumballs brought back good memories. Memories of putting a coin in a machine at a rundown mall as a child, and inevitably getting my least-favorite color every time.

My lips curved upward slightly.

Maybe the gumballs weren't a waste of space after all.

"I'm stuck wherever Rhett is, since no one else is willing to keep me warm without turning it into a *sharing* situation," I told Kyle and his gang.

All of the men looked at Rhett.

Refusing to move would probably help his case against staying on the island. But instead, he dipped his head. "It's about time to call it a night anyway."

When Rhett stood, I went with him, still leaning against his side. He left his arm over my shoulders, relaxingly heavy and blissfully warm.

The other guys chatted all the way back to the unfinished shelters, and through the plasticky, packaged brownie desserts we shared.

Everyone chewed gumballs while the conversation continued, and we'd barely made a dent in them when everyone turned in for the night.

Rhett and I took the far end of one of the shelters. Rain was still pouring down on us, and the leaves over our heads didn't do nearly as good a job of blocking the water as I would've hoped.

He settled on his back, with his side against Ev's. Like all the other men, he'd put his wings and horns away for the sake of sleeping, which meant I couldn't use them as an umbrella anymore.

But I'd survive.

He gestured me toward him when he was comfortable—or as comfortable as he could be on a lumpy bamboo platform while it rained.

After a moment of hesitation, the cold made up my mind for me.

I got cozy on my side, my front to Rhett's hip while I tried to press as much of my body to his as I could. I was so close to the edge of the shelter that it was a balancing act, but the fae were massive, so I'd expected that.

Luckily, one of them would be going home the next day. That would mean more space, I hoped.

"I usually sleep like a starfish," I whispered. "I'm sorry in advance if I end up sprawling over you during the night."

He grunted.

I felt bad, but not bad enough to try my luck with the harem.

So, I just closed my eyes and tried to sleep. I expected it to take a while, but I was out almost immediately.

four

RHETT

I STARED up at the dripping leaves, my heart beating steadily against Erin's. The woman had draped her entire body over mine within minutes of falling asleep. My cock was pinned beneath her thigh, her soft breasts were against my chest, and her head was tucked against my neck.

I shouldn't have wanted her, but I did. My erection made that impossible to deny. I could've called it nature, but I knew better.

It was her.

I hadn't been attracted to Molly or any of the other compatible females I'd guarded as they played in *Bachelorette*. But the moment I'd met Erin, she had my complete attention.

That didn't change anything, of course.

I had no intention of taking a mate.

It was just a distraction.

A pleasant one.

If I had to spend the last few weeks of my life playing in *Survival*, at least I would do so with an intriguing woman who smelled nice.

five

ERIN

THE FIRST THOUGHT to cross my mind when I woke up was that Rhett's cock was huge.

Huge, huge.

And nestled in the fold where my leg met my pelvis, thick and hard and way too close to my core.

Which was exactly where I wanted him, even if there wasn't a chance in hell I could admit that out loud.

His chest rose and fell steadily, his arms draped over my back and lower waist. I could feel how relaxed he was—in everywhere except that particular place—and knew he was really sleeping.

Rain was still dripping onto my back from the leaves that made up our roof, and I could still hear it falling.

So, we weren't done with that particular hell.

On the plus side, it was the perfect opportunity to work on those feelings Rhett had mentioned.

Wanting someone to share a bed with.

The horniness.

My face heated, my eyes still closed.

I needed to make myself want sex, and there was an obvious focus for that particular desire at the moment.

Rhett.

I let my thoughts linger on his cock, and considered what it might feel like if I shifted my weight a little.

Just enough to line him up with my center.

I imagined the feel of his thick erection against my clit.

His hands finding my ass and rocking me the way he wanted to, too.

His mouth taking mine, our bodies moving together, until—

One of Rhett's arms tightened around my upper back.

The other slid down to my ass, until a large hand was gripping one of my cheeks like he owned it.

My face burned.

Desire clenched my lower belly.

I didn't move.

Not when I was waiting for him to decide what he was going to do next.

A moment passed, then another.

And finally, he released me entirely. His erection throbbed against me violently.

I slipped off of him before opening my eyes and striding down the beach. My hands were shaking, so I shoved them in the pockets of my soaked running shorts. Rain was still falling hard, but I barely noticed it.

The zippers were scratchy against my wrists, and the pockets themselves were uncomfortably small.

I left my hands in them anyway.

The need in my lower belly didn't dissipate with the distance like I hoped it would. My guard had threatened any guys who tried flirting with me, so it had been years since I had sex—and apparently, now that it was an option again, my body liked the idea.

A lot.

I kept moving until I was far enough away that no one could see or hear me. Stepping behind a tree, I pressed my back up against it.

My chest rose and fell rapidly, the base of my palm pushing hard against my sternum.

I itched to put my hands between my thighs, but I knew Jordan was watching me, and wasn't interested in giving him a show.

On top of that, any of the men could come looking for me at any time. It was light enough that they'd be waking up soon, if they weren't already up.

As if to confirm my thoughts, Harker and Jim came walking up to me. They hadn't been in the shelter with me and Rhett, so I didn't think they'd seen the way I was laying on top of him.

"You okay, Erin?" Harker asked, a look on his face I couldn't read.

I was still breathing fast. "Yep."

He waited. I assumed he was waiting for an explanation.

Jim waited too.

"Just had an intense dream," I said.

Understanding dawned in Harker's eyes.

Jim's lips curved wickedly. "I can help with that."

Harker smacked him on the arm, but Jim didn't so much as flinch.

The bastard had just propositioned me, and we all knew it.

I didn't like him—but I couldn't get that mental image of me and Rhett out of my head.

And I didn't think Jim would actually go through with anything when he knew it would make him a target.

But... chaos.

I was there for chaos.

So, I nodded. "That would be great. Can you give us some space, Harker?"

Harker's eyes widened with disbelief. "No, that's—"

Jim's gleamed. "You heard the woman, Hark."

He strode toward me.

My stomach clenched tighter.

I didn't want Jim, but I did need to get my mind off Rhett...

And if he was actually willing...

Oh, who was I kidding?

I couldn't screw the guy. Not when I disliked him, and was attracted to Rhett.

But I could wreak a little havoc and make sure no one realized it was Rhett I had steamy dreams about.

"Jim," Harker warned.

"Fuck off." Jim set his hands on my hips. I didn't like having my back to a tree when he was the one pinning me, but I couldn't do anything about it without walking away from the opportunity. "Your pheromones smell delicious, Erin. Are they for me?"

"You tell me." I tipped my head back.

His eyes moved over my lips for a long moment before he leaned down and kissed me.

I'd been kissed before, though it had been more than four years since the last time. I had liked kissing. I'd kissed strangers in bars, and had one-night-stands that involved leaving before the men woke up.

But his lips made me rethink my past enjoyment.

The kiss was fine, but not spectacular.

He tasted *wrong*, somehow. I wasn't sure what the problem was, but there *was* a problem.

And while I knew I didn't want to keep kissing him, I didn't let myself pull away. Because finding a mate who wouldn't hurt me was crucial—and chaos was exactly what I needed to make that happen.

So, I buried my hands in his hair and went up on my tiptoes, pressing my front to his. His hands moved up my waist and over my breasts, squeezing one of them hard.

I grabbed his wrist and put his hand on my waist, silently telling him to quit groping me.

The kiss went on for a few minutes before Jim vanished.

I opened my eyes at the sudden loss, and blinked when I saw his back slam into a tree.

At first I thought it was Rhett moving him—but after a minute, I realized the man's haircut was wrong and his skin was a few shades different.

Ev.

Ev was the one who'd ripped Jim away from me.

Thank you, Ev.

"What the fuck, Jim?" Ev snarled. "We're all here competing for her, and you think grabbing her fucking tits is a good idea?"

"She offered," Jim said. "If you had the opportunity, you'd—"

"I'd tell her I'll make her mine in every fucking way after she's made me her mate. Touching someone else's woman is a damn good way to get yourself voted off, if you survive until the council," Ev snapped.

Despite the unpleasant taste of Jim in my mouth, I watched their interaction with rapture.

I'd done it.

I'd started the chaos.

And he'd mentioned my pheromones, so I must've ignited those when I got all lusty about Rhett.

Guess I just needed to fantasize about the grumpy bastard every night, and chaos would ensue.

Perfect.

The guys continued arguing, and I slipped away before they could bring me into the fight.

Though I wanted desperately to wash the scent of both my desire and Jim off my skin, I needed to leave it. The rain would remove enough of it—and whatever lingered would piss off the other guys, I hoped.

I passed a few other men heading toward the snarling males in the forest, but didn't slow until I reached the shelter area and sat down a few trees away from where Rhett was positioned. He was sitting down on his ass, his back to a tree.

Despite the chill in the air, my heart was beating fast enough that I wasn't cold.

I sat down two trees away from him, in case he could smell Jim's scent and it would bother him or something.

"What did you do, Chaos?" His voice was low enough that no one else might've heard.

I shrugged, fighting back a grin. "Nothing."

Rhett shook his head at me slowly.

Two men came jogging out of the forest, murder in their eyes.

"Did you fuck Jim?" one of them growled at me. It was Travis. He was with Ian, the new guy.

Maybe Travis wasn't as laid-back as I thought.

"Did I?" I let my eyes widen as if I didn't know what he was talking about.

Travis snarled, and Ian set a hand on his shoulder, though his expression was tight too.

"Let's get the story from the source," Ian said, much calmer.

"She *is* the—"

"Now," Travis's said sharply. Ian stiffened for a moment before both men headed into the forest.

"You were only in the jungle with him for five minutes," Rhett said. "Not long enough to fuck. And Harker was with you."

"Not long enough for *you* to fuck, maybe," I drawled.

He lifted an eyebrow at me. "Even if you climaxed in five *seconds*, we would only be getting started. A woman doesn't leave my bed until she's forgotten her own name."

If I hadn't been wet between my thighs before he said that, I definitely was after.

"Your plan was supposed to involve *flirting*. Not anything more physical than that. You don't want anyone to die."

"My plan was chaos," I corrected. "And no one will kill each other over what we did."

"If you did anything more than snuggle up with Jim, he'll come back bruised and bleeding."

I rolled my eyes, but I did remember Cameron burning his scent off Molly's skin after their hug.

And when Jim came back, he *was* bleeding.

Bruised, too.

And limping.

I bit my lip to hide my grimace.

Maybe Rhett was right. I needed to be sneaky about it if I decided to kiss anyone else.

Though, after the experience, I wasn't exactly dying to do so again.

THE REST of the day was tense.

And rainy.

No one spoke to me for more than a few seconds.

When the sun finally set, I was more than ready for one of the guys to leave.

The council area had been simple and bland in the first season, but we discovered that ours was nicer when we arrived. There were large wooden logs for benches, a massive canopy over our heads, and a fire burning in the center. The floor was some kind of wood planking, keeping us off the wet sand.

There were two comfortable-looking chairs across from the logs.

I sat down in one of them when Jordan gestured me toward it, and immediately lifted my soaked, wrinkled feet up toward the fire.

Dry, warm toes would feel amazing.

Jordan didn't waste any time with pleasantries, just passing out the voting papers and markers. When he said the word, everyone voted, and he collected all of the papers.

I watched, silently hoping a fight would break out or something, just so I could stay beneath the canopy and near the fire a little longer.

But, there was no fight.

And reading the votes didn't take long at all.

Jim.
Reid.
Jim.
Jim.
Jim.
Jim.
Jim.
Jim.
Jim.
Jim.
Jim.

The dragon bastard winked at me and blew a kiss before he sauntered out from beneath the canopy.

I wasn't at all sad to see him go.

And despite the blood and bruises I'd caused, one thing was clear:

I could influence the game through chaos while figuring out which of the men could stay controlled despite it.

And I intended to do exactly that.

. . .

THE MOOD WAS dark as everyone made their way back to the shelters. That was my fault, but I didn't feel bad about it.

They were playing a game for their lives, yes, but they had been given the opportunity to choose to play.

I hadn't.

When we called it a night, I followed Rhett back to the place we'd slept the last time. He hadn't snuggled to keep me warm that evening, but I hadn't needed him to. It hadn't been quite as cold as the night before.

"Is it still okay if I sleep next to you?" I asked him quietly, feeling many sets of eyes on me.

"As long as you scrub Jim's scent off your skin first."

Oh.

Considering the possessiveness he'd warned me about, that seemed fair.

I nodded, slipping down to the beach.

I didn't notice the man sitting on the sand until I was almost on top of him, and jumped when he waved.

"Dammit, Kyle," I hissed. "Don't surprise me like that."

He chuckled. "It wasn't intentional. Sorry."

"It's fine." I slipped into the water, only going in to my waist. It felt warmer than the air, despite the falling rain, so

I didn't mind.

It didn't take long to scrub myself down, including rinsing my mouth with the salt water just to be safe. Kyle was still sitting there when I emerged.

I waved at him on my way back up the beach, and he mirrored the motion.

The cold air and rain had me shivering by the time I got back to the shelter. There was sand stuck to my feet and legs, and I was regretting my agreement to get in the water.

When I reached Rhett, I curled up against his side without hesitation.

He grunted at the contact.

The jerk probably regretted sending me back to the water too.

But he didn't complain when I pressed more of my icy skin against his insanely warm side.

And once again, I fell asleep way too quickly.

ERIN

THE TENSION EASED over the next few days.

The rain didn't.

It got crazy windy a few times, enough so that it tore apart the leaves over the top of our shelters, but the men rebuilt them stronger with bamboo.

Waking up on top of Rhett's erection every day kept my pheromones from easing up, despite the utter misery of the rain, but the men were avoiding me too thoroughly to wreak more chaos.

So, I kept to myself.

It was kind of lonely.

Or a lot lonely.

And it gave me way too much time to think about the fantasies I kept having of me and Rhett.

That was going to be a problem in the long run if I couldn't stop it... but hopefully I'd move on. Because the last thing I needed was to choose a man who was going to turn me down at the end of the game.

But there was still plenty of game left.

Too much game left, in fact.

If there was a fast-forward button, you can be sure as hell that I would've pressed it.

ON THE AFTERNOON of day five, we were all packed in a speedboat like sardines, and hauled off to an island nearby.

When we saw a huge, square area full of what was undoubtedly mud, I grimaced.

Just what we needed—more of a mess.

The rain was still coming down endlessly. My skin was a wrinkled mess, cracked and bleeding in more than a few spots, and the only time I stopped shivering was when I was pressed up against Rhett at night.

It was already hellish.

Why not throw in a little mud to make it worse?

I slumped down on the bench provided for me, pulling my legs up and holding them against my chest as the men lined up in front of Jordan.

He was in just as terrible shape as the rest of us, though the fae seemed to be handling it better than I was.

"The second challenge is mud wrestling," Jordan said, flashing the guys a grin that looked genuine despite the hell we were all going through. "The top two will fly with Erin to a spa nearby, and spend more than twenty-four hours relaxing indoors, with all the food they can stomach."

"Indoors, as in, out of the rain?" Harker asked, eyes glittering with hope.

Maybe the guys *were* suffering as much as I was, minus the shivering.

"Yup," Jordan confirmed.

"What kind of food?" Rhett asked.

"We have chefs there to make whatever you want."

The steel that set into Rhett's eyes told me he was going to play this time.

A few guys exchanged grimaces.

They must've put that together too.

No one had told me much—they mostly avoided talking to me—but I'd gotten the impression that Rhett wasn't someone that anyone messed with. He was at least strong enough that he'd been chosen to guard Molly during her season.

Kyle grinned. "Let's get this show on the road."

The groans that echoed from two of the smaller guys said everyone knew who was going to win.

And sure enough, when the wrestling began, Kyle and Rhett destroyed everyone else. It wasn't even a competition.

An hour after the challenge began, Rhett had me crushed against his grumbling chest as he, Kyle, and Jordan took off from the beach.

I didn't mind at all, because I was *finally* going to get dry.

THE SPA WAS a small building just off the beach of a massive island. The building looked new enough for me to think the Society had paid to have it built themselves.

I didn't ask where in the world it was.

I didn't really care, honestly.

Just wanted to get out of the rain.

Rhett landed on the smooth porch, shifting his wings away as the roof over our heads protected us from falling water.

Jordan led us inside, and a friendly woman gave us a quick tour of the place.

There was a mud bath—hard pass—and a sauna—harder pass—in one room. Three massage tables in another.

A bedroom with a gigantic bed across from a large TV in a third.

A luxurious bathroom with a big jacuzzi tub and a bigger shower in a fourth.

My eyes landed on the towels first.

Fuck, I wanted to dry off, but they were clean and I was not.

"Go take a shower," Kyle said, waving me toward the bathroom. "We'll finish the tour and wait our turns."

"All there is left is a kitchen and small dining area," the woman said pleasantly. "It's not a problem to show Erin the way afterward."

"Thank you." Though my words were for her, my eyes were on Kyle.

I needed it.

Badly.

I'd shower fast, so they weren't waiting too long.

He dipped his head, and was still grinning when I shut the bathroom door behind me.

I ignored the hell out of the mirror, not wanting to see what I looked like. I didn't need it to know I looked like shit.

My sports bra, t-shirt, and running shorts were on the floor in a heartbeat, and I stepped beneath the falling water without waiting for it to warm up.

It heated quickly, and I fought a groan when I finally soaped up my hair and scrubbed the sand off my body.

Blissful.

It was blissful.

Though I enjoyed it, I really wanted to be dry, so I didn't stay in any longer than the time it took to get clean.

Stepping out, I couldn't suppress my groan when I wrapped myself in the towel.

The water was finally leaving my skin.

Finally.

I felt so good when I was done drying off, my hair up in a towel, that I almost cried.

Maybe I should chop my hair off before I went back into the game.

Did the spa have scissors anywhere?

I'd have to ask. Long hair was shit in constant rain. It dripped on me even more than the trees.

Anyway, there were three folded piles of clothing on the countertops, each with a nametag label over the top.

My fingers skimmed the fabric of mine.

A gray cotton underwear set, and a matching robe.

Perfect.

I pulled them on without hesitation, the dry fabric feeling luxurious on my skin.

It might've been the best day of my life.

The best day of my month, for sure. Maybe the best day of my year, considering how shitty things had been.

After giving myself a minute to take it all in, I finally slipped out of the bathroom and walked toward the smell of cooking food.

I found Kyle chatting with Jordan at a four-person dining table. All three men had large plates in front of them, and though the plates were empty, there were signs that there had been food on them at some point.

"Sorry, I tried to be quick," I said, taking the empty seat. There was no plate in front of it, but I could hear food sizzling behind a door nearby.

"No need to apologize. We've been having a good time," Kyle said, patting his chiseled abdomen. "The chef is fucking fantastic. Go ahead, Rhett."

Rhett left silently.

I couldn't stop my gaze from tracking him out of the room.

"You like him," Kyle said, as soon as Rhett was gone.

I didn't answer, assuming he was talking to Jordan about whatever they'd been discussing earlier.

"Erin," he said.

"Hmm?" I looked over.

"You like him. Rhett." He nodded in the direction Rhett had gone.

My face heated, though I tried to prevent it. "Bullshit."

Kyle grinned. "I was awake the morning your pheromones started. They started because of him."

"Like hell they did."

He laughed. "Don't bother denying it. I'm on your side here."

I scoffed. "You're competing to win me like a prize, asshole."

"If it was that simple, I would've won the last season." His grin widened. "I'm competing to get to the end. You might be the prize, but you're also the only one who awards it."

"So?"

"I got to the end with Cameron and Molly. I've figured out how this game works." He nodded toward me. "So, we should make a truce."

"A *truce*?" My voice raised, slightly incredulous.

"A truce," he agreed. "I'll do what I can to get Rhett to the end, and continue convincing everyone that he's not a risk for as long as I can. In exchange, if you can't convince him that you're worth staying alive for, you pick me."

"Why would you ever agree to that?"

"Because I've been friends with Rhett for a long-ass time, and I don't want to watch the bastard fade when there's a woman interested in him. And if he doesn't mate with you, I don't think he's living long enough to play another round."

My stomach clenched. "He doesn't want me."

"He doesn't know what he wants. Hasn't since Kellie broke his heart. Give him a reason to live, and he'll be the best fucker you could ask for. You've seen how much the other guys on the island respect him. You know that's true."

"I don't know him well enough to make a decision like that right now."

Kyle nodded. "I get it. You can take some time to think about it; I won't tell anyone what I've realized. Let me know when you make up your mind."

The door to the kitchen opened, and a new woman came out with three massive plates of food. She smiled at all of us, not batting an eye at Rhett's absence, and left the food with the three of us.

The conversation ended as we dug in.

And damn, I could get used to staying at the spa.

RHETT RETURNED before I'd finished my plate. He took Kyle's seat and remaining food.

After sharing an island and eating off leaves while rain poured on us for days, a few germs were the least of our worries.

"Enjoy," Kyle called over his shoulder as he left. "I'm going to take a long-ass bath. Don't wait up."

We ate in silence until the food was gone, then leaned back in our chairs. With my belly so full, I was starting to get tired.

"So, Chaos," Rhett said, his voice rough in a way I loved.

I needed to stop loving it, but that didn't change the situation any.

"So, Rhett," I drawled.

His lips curved upward just the tiniest bit. It was like the laughter I'd gotten out of him a few times—so quiet, it was hard to identify.

"You never told me why you were so focused on wreaking havoc. Or why you stopped."

"I *paused* because of the rain," I said. "It's hard to come up with brilliant plans while you're suffering."

"Of course."

"And you never told me why you're so against taking a mate after the last one broke your heart."

I watched for a flinch, waiting for a reaction, but Rhett didn't seem triggered at all by my words.

He just studied me.

It made me feel kind of naked, even though I was damn sure I was wearing a gloriously soft robe.

Finally, he dipped his head. "Most of the guys would tell you I'm still in love with her. Kellie."

"I'm not asking most of the guys."

"You're not," he agreed. "And I'm not in love with her.

Haven't been for a long time. She was disgusted by what I was. I was too, for a while."

"Then why are you against it?"

His gaze lingered on the wall behind me. I itched to look back, to see if there was a painting or something, but didn't want to risk shutting him up by doing so.

"It was always a battle," he finally said. "I'd ask her what she wanted for dinner, she'd tell me she didn't care, and then she'd be upset that I hadn't realized she wanted Chinese. She'd ask me to plan a special date night, I'd spend a few hours trying to come up with romantic shit, and she'd be disappointed when we got home because what I planned wasn't what she'd envisioned."

He let out a long breath. "The way I folded her laundry when I did it with mine wasn't exactly how she wanted it. The food I made for dinner wasn't what she happened to be craving. I woke up too early on the weekdays. Too late on the weekends. I made more money than her, which bothered her, but when I tried to pay for things, she insisted I was insulting her. The only thing we weren't shit at was sex."

If he was anywhere near as good as my fantasies, I didn't have a problem believing that much.

"So, the summary of your reasoning is…" I trailed off, wanting to hear him explain his thoughts.

"I don't want to spend eternity like that," he said bluntly. "When she threw the engagement ring at me and walked away, it hurt—but I was relieved. So fucking relieved. I'd rather fade than land myself in another relationship."

Well, that was... not what I was expecting him to say.

"I'm not exactly the poster-child for safe, happy relationships, but you do know that it's not always like that, right? There's therapy. There's learning how to communicate. If she had been willing, you could've gotten there."

He shook his head. "Not with her."

"She obviously wasn't the right person for you. But just because she was shitty, doesn't mean all women are. Letting yourself die because you're afraid to risk more pain seems like the coward's way out to me.

Anger flooded his eyes. "I'm not *afraid*."

I lifted an eyebrow. "You got thrown off the horse, and you didn't get back on. It's absolutely your right not to, but don't lie to yourself. Fear is fear."

"You don't understand," Rhett bit out.

I laughed humorlessly. "I grew up watching my mom's boyfriend abuse her in every way. *Experiencing* him abuse me, too. I'm *Chaos* because I have no choice but to marry a stranger, and I'm fucking terrified that I'm going to end up paired off with someone just like the monster who haunts my childhood. If a little havoc weeds out a few of the weaker men, then yeah, I'm going to wreak as much as possible." I stood up, pushing my chair back as I did. "I'm calling it a night. Enjoy your food."

With that, I left him at the table alone.

Jordan had to follow me.

Part of me hoped that Rhett would too, but he stayed where he was, undoubtedly still pissed off that I'd called him out for being scared.

He could be as angry as he wanted—he wasn't the one who was being forced to mate with someone he didn't know. Someone who was bigger and stronger than him in every single way.

My fingers still itched for scissors, to chop through the wavy mass of my hair, but staying up to cut it would likely lead to another conversation with Rhett.

So, I let myself retreat.

seven

RHETT

"STOP PACING," Kyle grumbled at me from where he was sprawled out on the opposite side of the bed from Erin. His voice was low, but we'd both realized by then that she slept like a rock no matter what was going on around her. The food coma after dinner would only make her sleep harder. "And tell me what she said to piss you off so much."

I gritted my teeth. "She thinks I'm afraid of relationships."

That wasn't what had me pacing.

It hadn't taken me long to realize she was right. And I wasn't angry with *her* for that. If anything, I was grudgingly glad she'd pointed it out.

What had me pacing was the realization that she was Kellie's exact opposite. Bluntly honest. Straight and to the point. Not dramatic in the slightest. There was no passive-aggression. Just aggression. Which was fucking *perfect*.

And on top of that? Her past.

Because the idea of a man hurting her?

It made me want to hunt the fucker down and kill him, slowly and painfully. He wouldn't be the first person I'd tortured, but he'd be the first whose pain I relished.

I trusted Kyle for the most part, but he didn't need to know her past.

He didn't *get* to know her past.

She was mine.

Or she *felt* like mine, though I knew she was nowhere near that.

Kyle snorted. "You *are* afraid of relationships."

"I know."

"So accept it and move on. Fight for her."

"You know damn well that if I show a shred of interest or possessiveness for the woman, I'll be off the island in a heartbeat," I growled.

He flashed me a white-toothed grin. "Unless you play the game my way."

"How?"

"Win."

I scoffed.

"Think about it, Rhetti. No one believes you're interested in taking a mate. You just have to fight your possessiveness enough to keep them thinking that way."

I was so pissed, the obnoxious nickname he'd been using for centuries didn't even register.

"She wants to cause chaos," I said flatly. "You think I can sit back and pretend not to be affected the next time she kisses some asshole in the jungle? It took everything I had not to kill Jim when I smelled him on her skin. If he'd been close enough, I would've done it."

Kyle's grin widened. "She can cause chaos without getting physical with anyone."

"How do you figure that?"

"She starts rumors. Walks around with a hickey on her neck, with her scent mysteriously washed clean. Someone will inevitably mention that they saw her leave a few minutes after someone else, and then the gossip will begin."

"You think I can let someone else mark her neck? We're not even together, and the idea pisses me off."

"*You* mark her neck, moron."

I kept pacing.

He watched me, waiting.

Though the bed was massive, Erin was already starfished across it, taking up eighty percent of the mattress. Her right hand was only a few inches away from Kyle's arm.

I itched to move it further.

"I shouldn't even be talking about this with you," I finally growled, running a hand through my curls. They weren't tangled, for the first time since I landed on the island. "You could tell everyone else that I want her."

"*Do* you want her?"

"I don't fucking know."

Kyle laughed. "Like hell you don't. And I told you from the beginning that we were allied, whether you liked it or not."

"That doesn't mean a damn thing in this game."

"Sure it does. And beyond the game, we're friends, Rhetti. Even if you sometimes wish we weren't. And friends don't let friends die when there's a woman they're finally considering living for."

"That's not convincing."

"The woman wants *you*," he said.

"I don't know that."

He lifted an eyebrow at me. "Her pheromones kicked in when she was pressed against you. I was right there. Her scent is there to pull *you* in. Not me. And for the record, I think I deserve a woman who actually likes me. You can have this one."

I grimaced.

He wasn't wrong on either front.

"You're really going to help me get to the end?"

"Sure am." He winked. "I've got a few more months in me. You don't."

"What do you want in exchange?"

"Nothing."

His response wasn't convincing.

Not at all.

I gave him a deadpanned stare, and he finally gave me a sheepish grin. "After the game's over, I need your help finding a male who can both handle my sister and treat her well. She wants to settle down, but you know most of the males find her intimidating."

She was.

Kyle's sister was a handful.

I knew a few men who would get along with her, though. It would be a pain in the ass, but I'd find someone.

"It's a reasonable request. You have a deal," I agreed.

His grin widened further. "Good. Now get in this bed before your female starts snuggling with me. She keeps creeping closer, and I'd like to make it through the night with my head attached to my body."

I was across the room and maneuvering my way beneath Erin's limbs in a heartbeat.

And despite the fury still coursing through my veins at her admission about her childhood, I was breathing more deeply than I'd been able to in months.

Because I was going to fight for Erin, even if it forced me to face everything I was apparently afraid of.

eight

ERIN

RHETT WAS BREATHING STEADILY beneath me when I woke up. Kyle was climbing out of our gigantic, shared bed, and the rustling blankets woke me even though I didn't feel the mattress dip.

Being draped over Rhett's body like a blanket probably prevented that.

I lifted my head, bleary eyes landing on Kyle.

He whispered, "I'm going to make myself at home in the mud bath. See you in a few hours."

I blinked, and he was gone.

Rhett's erection throbbed against my hip, and my face flushed.

I shouldn't have been attracted to him after our tense conversation the night before, but I was. And Kyle's ridiculous offer lingered in my mind.

He would get Rhett to the end, if I was willing to risk Rhett rejecting me when I chose him.

It was insane.

Ridiculous.

And yet some part of me had been ready to agree immediately.

That part of me was clearly lacking in common sense, because *come on*. What self-respecting woman would choose a man she knew would reject her? I'd been through enough shit in my life to know better.

But knowing better didn't change that ready-and-willing part of me.

Which was frustrating.

Wanting to avoid another tense conversation, I started to move carefully off of Rhett. His erection was still throbbing slowly, scrambling my mind a little and making my cheeks hot.

I ignored that as I put one knee on the mattress.

His hands on my waist, big and heavy, tightened.

I froze, breathing in and out steadily in an attempt to keep him from waking up.

A minute passed.

Then another.

His grip didn't loosen, but he was still enough that I didn't think I'd woken him.

I finally planted a hand beside my knee on the mattress and lifted the other half of my body, rolling away as smoothly as I could when I did.

My chest rose and fell quickly after I landed on my back, relief rolling through me.

No tense conversation.

No awkwardness.

No—

I sucked in a breath when a chiseled body rolled over the top of *me*.

Rhett's eyes were heavy with sleep, but he held his weight off of me so the pressure was nothing but comfortable. I waited for the position to trigger the trauma of my past, but it didn't happen. Something about the way he looked at me ensured that.

"You're trying to get away from me," he said.

"I need to pee."

It wasn't a lie.

I *did*.

That just wasn't the main reason I was bailing.

"You wouldn't have tried to be sneaky if that was it."

"I was being polite by trying not to wake you up," I tossed back. "Since I made myself at home on top of you while we were sleeping, I knew I'd bothered you enough."

His lips curved upward just the tiniest bit.

I hated how much I loved his soft smiles.

"Having you on top of me isn't a bother."

"Liar."

He lowered his pelvis over mine, lightly pressing his erection against me. "My body can't lie."

My face flushed. "A physical response isn't proof of anything. You'd be hard if a cat was laying on your cock."

He snorted.

The sound threw me off, it was so unexpected.

"I'm not a human teenager, Erin. I don't get hard unless I want something."

"And that something is..." I shot back, before I could reconsider pushing his buttons like that.

"You. Obviously." He shifted positions, easing his hips away from my core.

"Wanting me physically while we're playing a game that will require me to mate with someone else is bullshit," I said, fighting like hell to stop myself from wrapping my legs around his hips to pull him back to me.

"That's not possible."

My forehead creased.

"Wanting you and accepting that you'll mate with someone else," he clarified.

"You're too afraid to even consider taking a mate, so—"

"What if I wasn't?"

I blinked.

What if he *what*?

"What if I decided to face my fear?"

My body flushed.

I was already wet between my thighs, but the wetness increased.

"I'd say it doesn't matter, because I'm not interested in you."

It was a bold-faced lie.

The fire that blazed to life in his eyes told me he knew it, too.

"So you don't want me," Rhett said, his voice suspiciously calm.

"No." My heart was beating erratically.

"Then why did your pheromones kick in while you were on top of me?"

Crap.

Shit.

Damn.

"I was staring at someone else," I lied.

"Staring isn't enough to start them."

"Fine, I was *fantasizing* about someone else."

"Who?"

"I don't owe you an explanation," I snapped.

"You don't," he agreed. "But I'm not moving until I get one."

He lowered his hips just a little, and I sucked in a breath at the pressure against me.

He felt incredible.

I wanted more—*needed* more.

But I couldn't let myself have it.

"Fine," I said.

"Good." He lowered his forehead to rest against mine, his gigantic cock still pressing against my clit. I would get hornier the longer he stayed in that position, but I couldn't bring it up. Not without letting him win.

So, I waited.

A minute passed.

And another.

And another.

My breathing picked up, my heartbeat following suit.

My clit started throbbing the way his cock had.

I needed more.

Needed *him*.

"Tell me what I was doing to you in this fantasy," he murmured.

I bit my lip to stop myself from groaning.

"Unless you'd rather see what we did in mine."

My legs hooked around his waist of their own volition.

I squeezed my eyes shut, trying to force them to let go, but it didn't work. I wanted him too damn much.

"Show me." I couldn't stop the words from slipping out.

My mind spun for a moment—and when it righted itself, we were on the *Survival* island again.

The rain fell lightly, and I was draped over his body. The shelter was empty around us, his erection nestled between my thighs exactly how I wanted it.

The smell of what had to be his desire filled my lungs.

The wetness between my legs had me shifting slightly, moving against him.

His hands were on my ass, his grip light but unmistakably possessive as he slipped his hands beneath the light, damp fabric of my shorts and built-in panties.

I sucked in an unsteady breath at his grip on my backside.

Though it didn't feel entirely real—I could tell it wasn't actually happening—it was real *enough*.

He kneaded my ass slowly for a few minutes, his touch encouraging my movements as I rocked lightly against his cock. When my breathing was uneven, my abdomen tight with need, his fingers finally slid up my center.

I gasped when he dragged them through my wetness, over my clit.

"You're already ready for me." He nipped lightly at my ear.

"Yes," I breathed. "I need you now."

He slid a finger inside me, and I moaned softly.

"Louder, Chaos. I want every man on this island to know who you belong to." He added a second finger, and I cried out as he stretched me, still toying with my clit too. "You're too fucking tight. It'll take time to—"

"No." I pressed my forehead to his neck, arching my hips until the head of his cock was pressed against my slit, forcing the fabric of my shorts inside me with him and pinning his fingers down. "Take me now, or I'll get myself off with my fingers."

Rhett growled, but didn't waste any time.

He had my shorts pulled to the side in a heartbeat, and the thick head of his cock was pressing into my opening a moment later.

I cried out loudly as he pushed inside, just an inch.

"You're too tight," he gritted out. "You need—"

"More." I lowered my hips, forcing him the rest of the way inside me. In reality, it might've hurt a little—but in the fantasy, it was pure pleasure.

My climax hit, *hard,* and in reality.

I gasped as my release ended the illusion immediately, my hips rocking to drag out the bliss.

Rhett's chest was rumbling, his eyes dilated as I came down from the high. He'd rolled us both over during the illusion, so I was on top of him again. "That was the sexiest fucking thing I've ever seen."

"Bullshit," I panted.

His grip on my hips tightened further. "You don't believe me?"

"You told me yesterday that the sex between you and Kellie was amazing. That wasn't even sex. It's not possible for that to be the sexiest thing you've ever seen."

His eyes darkened. "I said it was the only thing we weren't shit at. Kellie didn't know what I was. I couldn't use my magic on her. She never saw my fae form or touched my wings. Every time we were together, I was at war with myself the entire time. So yes, watching you get off against my cock to nothing but the illusion I'm placing in your mind is the sexiest fucking thing I've ever seen."

If I hadn't already been flushed, I definitely was after hearing that. "You changed your tune fast, considering you were pissed at me for pointing out that you're afraid yesterday."

"I wasn't pissed at you. I was frustrated with myself for not realizing the truth sooner. And fucking furious with your mother's boyfriend. What's his name?"

"Matthew Olgden."

Rhett's nostrils flared.

"He died in the war," I said, eyeing him.

Rhett scowled. "One of the bombs?"

"Yep. Took my mom too. They were on vacation together."

"The fucker deserved much worse."

"On that, we agree."

Rhett slid his hand over my hip. "You believe me?"

"Mostly."

His eyes narrowed. "Mostly?"

"I have a hard time believing you considered her your mate even though you could never be yourself with her."

His forehead smoothed for the most part. "That was the easiest way to explain the shitshow to the other fae I interact with. In human terms, I proposed too soon. Her family was pushing it, and I couldn't explain my resistance without telling them what I was. We'd only been engaged a few days when I realized I had to tell her the truth before the planning went any further."

"How did you tell her? And how did she respond?"

He studied me for a moment before saying, "I can show you, if you want."

The illusions.

Right.

That was a handy trick, honestly.

I nodded, and my vision did the typical shift before everything changed.

We were standing in an old-fashioned apartment with stark gray walls and uncomfortable furniture made up of harsh lines.

The woman in front of us was tall and skinny, her smooth, highlighted blonde hair tied up in a severe bun. Her light skin was tanned, though it didn't look quite natural. Her expression was tight, her pretty face caked in makeup, and her lips painted in a perfectly-chosen neutral shade that complimented her complexion.

"Alright, I have a few minutes," Kellie said in a clipped voice. "What do you want to talk about?

"Let's sit down." Rhett took her arm lightly and led her over to an uncomfortable-looking couch, where they both sat. "I don't know how to tell you this," he admitted.

She tensed.

She probably thought he was going to admit to cheating or something, with that shitty introduction.

Note to self: Rhett was not great at starting important discussions.

"I'm not human," he said.

She blinked.

Her forehead creased.

"I'm fae," he said. "The legends about faeries started with us, though they have most things wrong." He rolled his shoulders lightly, and shifted to his fae form. His massive horns curled off his head, his wings spreading behind him.

Kellie went pale, fast.

Rhett reached for her arm when she swayed a little, but she moved it away before he could touch her.

"Get out," she said softly.

He shifted back to his human form. "Kellie, I—"

"Get out," she repeated. "I'll call you when I'm ready to talk."

The scene shifted.

Rhett was knocking on her door. The scruff on his face and tension in his position told me it had been a few days.

Kellie opened the door, her expression cold and hard. "What do you want?"

"You didn't call." Rhett's voice was low, but controlled. He was holding tightly to his emotions, careful not to let go. "It's been a

week, Kellie. You just posted that our engagement is over on social media, but didn't fucking call."

"You can't expect me to marry a monster," she shot back. "If I'd known what you were from the beginning, I never would've dated you at all." Leaving the door open, she stepped back for a moment and grabbed a diamond ring off something just inside the door.

She flung it at him, and he caught it as she slammed the door shut.

The illusion disappeared, and I stared down at Rhett. Though I expected the memories to upset him at least a little, he didn't look bothered. I didn't know if he was just hiding his emotions or if he genuinely wasn't hurt anymore.

"Wow," I said.

"Yeah."

"How does all that shit make you feel now?" I asked.

"Like I dodged a bullet."

"Or a bomb." I propped myself up on his chest. Though my robe had fallen loose during the night, my comfortable underwear hadn't budged. Good old granny panties and unsupportive cotton bra. "I'm not like her."

"Not even a little."

"You loved her."

"I loved not being alone."

"You were lonely?"

"Tremendously," he admitted. "I've never handled being alone well. Cameron was my closest friend, and he'd started fading. I was on my own too much. She pursued me, and the attention felt like what I needed. It wasn't until after she ended it that I realized how much I preferred the loneliness to being with the wrong person."

"And you don't think I'm another wrong person." It wasn't a question—it was a statement. The same one he'd made, but rephrased.

"I think you're the right person, actually."

"Why?" I wanted to hear his reasoning. Hell, I *needed* to if I was going to consider letting things go any further between us. Let alone agreeing to mate with him for the rest of our lives.

"You don't pretend to be anything you're not, and you don't take anyone's shit. On top of that, you're stunningly beautiful, as well as fearless, Chaos."

I rolled my eyes, though the gesture was half-hearted. No one had ever complimented me like that. It felt nice. Really nice. "I'm not fearless."

"Maybe not, but you don't let your fear control you. Any of the men in the game would be lucky to have you. What you should really be asking, is why you should want *me*."

"Tell me, then."

His lips curved upward. "Since my engagement ended, I've worked for the Society in keeping the peace. Before the war, when there was a fight, they sent me in. When a new compatible mate was found and chaos broke out, they called me. After the game shows began, they did the same. I kept the peace through season after season of *Bachelorette* before *Survival* began, and naturally, was brought in for this game considering its volatile nature."

Rhett continued "I don't hurt anyone unless I have to do so to protect someone else. I don't lose my temper. Everyone on the island would vouch for that. Yes, I would be intensely possessive if you were mine—but that would ensure your safety above anything else. No chaos required."

I bit my lip.

His gaze landed on my mouth, and lingered for a long moment. "I'll even tell you something, despite knowing it will lessen my chances with you."

"What is it?"

He chuckled, lifted his head, and murmured into my ear, "It's not possible for a male fae to physically hurt his bonded mate, or the other way around. Mated fae live for each other."

My heart beat painfully. "Are you sure?"

"Positive."

Well...

That changed things.

A lot of things.

I didn't need to cause chaos at all if the men would be equally unable to hurt me. I could choose a mate based solely on his personality.

Assuming my damn heart let me consider anyone other than Rhett. I still didn't know why I was so interested in him. Maybe because he was so good at snuggling.

ERIN

"YOU SAID Kellie never touched your wings," I said, changing the subject so I didn't have to talk about choosing a mate anymore. That shit was stressful. "Are wings sensitive?"

"They are."

"*How* sensitive."

"On the same level as my cock."

My eyebrows shot upward. "Has *anyone* ever touched them?"

"No." He brushed a few strands of hair from my eyes.

Somehow, we'd sidestepped into another intimate conversation.

Some part of me wanted to climb back out, but that part wasn't at the forefront of my mind. Not even close.

"If we mated, you'd let me?" I asked.

He chuckled. "I'd let you now if you wanted to."

I wasn't sure why, but I *did* want to.

Maybe I wanted physical evidence that I would treat him better than Kellie had if he gave me the chance.

Maybe I wanted to distract myself from the serious conversation about choosing a permanent mate.

Or maybe I was just a little possessive too, and wanted to claim some part of him no one else ever had.

Unlike him, I had no magical fading to blame the possessiveness on. So, I wasn't admitting to anything.

"Shift," I said.

Rhett adjusted his position on the bed slightly, moving down the mattress and raising his shoulders just enough as he changed. His wings spread behind him, horns curved from his head, and his body grew a bit.

His erection did, too.

Whew, that was hot.

"Can we even fuck when you're this big?" I asked him, earning a small but wicked smile.

"After we're mated, yes. We'd have to be careful, before."

I guess my body would adjust for his if we sealed a bond. Becoming fae myself would probably do that for me.

Leaning forward, I wrapped my hand around one of his horns. His eyes closed, and he let out a breath.

"How does that feel?" I asked him, watching his reactions.

"Nice. Similar to a scalp rub."

"When I'm fae, I won't have horns?"

"No. Female fae don't have them."

I dragged my thumb slowly over the tip, and earned a murmured curse. "Fuck me, that's good."

My lips curved upward slightly.

It had been a long, long time since I'd been with a man, but it had always made me feel powerful. The knowledge that I could bring pleasure to a guy as strong as Rhett was intoxicating.

Releasing his horn, I lowered my hand to the smooth surface of his wing. My fingers brushed the center of it lightly, just to the right of his bicep.

His whole body tensed, his cock throbbing hard against my center.

"How is it?" I moved my fingers again.

He swore loudly, grabbing my wrist with the hand furthest from me and holding my fingers where they were. "Stop, Chaos."

I started to pull my hand away, but he held it in place.

"I'm going to release all over your only set of clean clothes if you keep going." He gritted the words out.

I looked down at the robe and exposed panties.

Did I care?

If I weren't playing *Survival*, I wouldn't have batted an eye. But dry, clean clothes were a rarity on the island.

"Take them off me," I said.

His eyes opened, gaze hot, heavy, and a little suspicious.

Like he didn't believe I meant it, which was just plain ridiculous. I never said anything I didn't mean. In fact, I usually said *too much* of what I meant.

"If you're going to cover me in your pleasure, wouldn't you rather coat my bare skin anyway?" I asked.

Fire burned in his eyes. "I should get you off again first."

"Why? I'll probably climax again with you. You'll still be between my thighs, right?"

He growled. "Yes."

"Then don't make me wait any longer."

He tugged the tie around my waist undone, and I lifted my hand off his wing so he could push the robe's sleeves down my arms. His hands slid slowly over my breasts, his grip gentle.

Too gentle.

"I'm not going to break, Rhett. If you're going to touch me, *touch me.*"

"You're perfect." His voice was low as he worked my breasts harder through my bra.

I dragged my fingers lightly against his wings again.

He had my bra over my head in a heartbeat, and gripped my bare breasts. I inhaled sharply, loving both the feel of it and the heat in his eyes.

When his hands left my tits, they slid down my hips and to my panties. He tugged the fabric down my thighs, lifting my legs one at a time. The motion was a little awkward, but the moment wasn't. The way he watched me said he liked stripping me down as much as I liked having him do so.

When he lowered my leg back to his side, it set my core against his erection. There was nothing between us but his shorts.

"We shouldn't ruin your only pair of clothes either," I said, heart beating quickly.

It was a fair point, but honestly?

I just wanted to feel him against me.

He lifted us both off the mattress long enough to tug the fabric down his legs.

I sucked in a breath at the heat of his bare cock against my clit. He throbbed, and my hips arched.

"Easy," he warned, one of his hands wrapping possessively around my hip while the other slid back up to my breast and squeezed.

"Easy is boring," I breathed, stroking his wing again until he was throbbing hard beneath me.

"No part of being with me will ever be boring, Chaos. Slow down so this can last."

The last bit was an order—maybe the first order he'd ever given me.

I liked it more than I wanted to admit.

"How dominant are you in bed?" I asked him, forcing myself not to move anymore so we could slow it down the way he wanted.

"As dominant as you want me to be."

I scowled. "No, Rhett. How dominant are *you*?"

His eyes flashed. "I don't know. I've never let go of control enough to find out."

The wetness between my thighs increased dramatically. "Let's find out, then."

I started to move my hips lightly, but a knock at the door had me freezing.

Was it locked?

What if Kyle was back earlier than he'd planned?

We—

"Breakfast is ready," a pleasant female voice said. "And your massage therapists are waiting in the room. Kyle's still in the mud bath, and would prefer you go without him."

I opened my mouth to tell her we weren't hungry, or that we'd eat later.

But my mind went back to Rhett saying he wasn't sure how dominant he was.

That he had never let himself find out.

So... maybe I couldn't abandon my chaos just yet.

Closing my mouth, I let him decide for us.

Rhett's jaw was clenched.

He hadn't gotten off, so it'd be a lot shittier for him than me if we stopped.

A minute passed.

Then another.

He watched me, waiting for me to make up my mind.

Instead, I shrugged.

"We're coming," he finally told the woman. Lowering his voice, he said, "I should feed you."

I didn't tell him that the only thing I wanted him to *feed me* was his cock.

I needed to figure out exactly who he was and how much he chose to fight his needs and desires. And I needed to do it *before* I committed to anything with him. Before I let myself take charge the way I wanted to, too.

Because I wasn't going to spend an eternity mated to someone who refused to fight for what he wanted—or even to *tell me* what he wanted.

We'd already made progress on that front, but everything was new.

Really new.

So... I had to let him take charge for a bit, even if it wasn't natural for me.

I slid off his erection, and his grip tightened for a moment before he released me.

Climbing off the bed, I let myself look at him for a moment.

He was gigantic.

Those monstrous wings and massive horns were beautiful, in their own way. His chiseled muscles were perfect—that much was undebatable. And his cock?

Damn.

He sat up without mentioning the way I was staring at him. A quick glance at his face told me his eyes were on my body the way mine had been on his, hence his lack of acknowledgement.

Forcing my gaze off him, I found my robe on the edge of the bed and slipped it over my shoulders. I was tying it around my middle when Rhett stepped beside me and held out my bra and panties.

"I don't need those," I said, grabbing them and tossing them onto the mattress.

It was time to push him a little.

His forehead creased. "Why not?"

"We're getting massages. I'm not wearing underwear through it. A robe is easy to take off."

His nostrils flared.

That was anger.

He didn't like the idea of me being naked during a massage?

Interesting.

"We're having breakfast first," he said.

"So?"

His nostrils flared again. "Kyle could come back to the room and find them."

I lifted an eyebrow. "And that's a problem because..."

"Because you're mine, Erin." His fist tightened on the fabric.

If he had asked or even ordered me to put them on, I would've done it. I honestly would've rather worn them than waltz around the spa in nothing but a thin cotton robe. Everyone there would see the outline of my tits through the fabric, and the chance of flashing more was high.

But, for the sake of chaos, I'd play.

"Am I?" I asked.

"*Yes.*"

The woman knocked on the door again.

Rhett clenched his jaw, and tucked the undergarments in his pocket. I was a little disappointed he hadn't stood up for how he felt and what he wanted, but I didn't say as much.

He didn't take my hand as he strode to the door, or as he pulled it open for me.

I didn't offer it.

I was still waiting to see whether or not he was willing to fight for me. It was one thing to say he wanted me when we were horny in bed together, but it was something else entirely to act like it when there were other people around.

Our arms brushed as he stepped into place beside me on the way to the kitchen, but otherwise we didn't touch. I could feel Jordan's attention on us, and caught a glimpse of his curiosity when I did, but I wasn't about to clarify anything.

That bastard was there for the Society, not for me.

BREAKFAST WAS FINE. The food was amazing, and I once again ate enough to make myself sick.

Rhett's eyes were on me the whole time, but he didn't try to start a conversation, so I didn't either.

After we were done, they led us to the massage room. One of the three tables had been removed, so there was just one for each of us. One male therapist, and one female, too.

Both looked friendly, and were attractive for humans.

Though some part of me immediately wanted to take the table in front of the woman so she wouldn't have her hands on Rhett's skin, I had a role to play.

So, I strode right over to the guy's table and flashed him a smile.

He returned it.

There was a growl a few feet away, but I didn't look over. Pushing him to make up his mind was kind of the point.

The humans excused themselves so we could undress, and I finally let myself look over at Rhett.

His eyes were narrowed. "*No*, Erin."

My body warmed.

I fought a smile of triumph and lifted an eyebrow. "He's human, Rhett. He's not even competing."

"I don't give a fuck who he is. The only man who puts his hands on you is me."

"Fine." I untied my robe and slid it off my shoulders.

His eyes ran slowly over my figure, his chest rumbling low.

The sound was almost appreciative.

I half expected him to hand me the underwear and order me to put them back on, but he didn't.

So, I slipped beneath the sheet on the table.

He strode to my side and pulled it up higher, until it covered my shoulders entirely.

"You know she's going to move it around during the massage," I said.

"I know." The words were nearly another growl.

But instead of fighting it, he stripped his pants off and walked to his own table, erection still jutting out. It almost looked painful.

"Are your balls blue yet?"

"You have no idea." He grunted as he settled on the table face-down. His wings and horns were long gone, but he was still a little too big for the table. "Knowing you're naked beneath a sheet isn't going to help a damn thing."

"I can start fantasizing again too, if you want," I teased.

I wouldn't really.

As much as I wanted to wreak havoc, I didn't want to make the humans uncomfortable. I knew that feeling far too much to wish it on them. We were powerless compared to the fae.

Or *they* were, I supposed.

I had a whole island of men competing to become my mate. That made me pretty damn powerful.

"Don't even think about it." His voice made me warm.

"Or what?" I tossed back.

The massage therapists knocked on the door and stepped inside before he could answer.

As I got comfortable, the briefest flicker of an illusion flashed through my mind.

Me, bent over the edge of the table while he drove into me from behind, pinning my hands beneath his.

I grinned into the table.

My plan was totally going to get his dominance out, and then we were *really* going to have fun.

ERIN

UNFORTUNATELY, Jordan announced it was time to head out as soon as the massages were over. The massage therapists left us to get dressed, and my guard turned his back to us, studiously looking away.

Someone had cleaned our island clothes and left them folded on a table beside my robe, so I headed for them instead. The robe wasn't exactly great for sand, beaches, or rain.

I stepped into my running shorts, then reached for my sports bra. Before I grabbed it, Rhett caught my hands.

His eyes leveled with mine. "We need to talk."

My stomach clenched even though I knew it couldn't have been that bad of a conversation.

Shit, he was terrible with introductions. We needed to chat about that.

"How long until we leave?" I asked Jordan.

"You've got about five minutes," he said, without turning toward us.

Five minutes wasn't great.

"I made a deal with Kyle," he said.

I blinked.

Kyle made a deal with *both* of us?

Bastard.

"I'm going to continue acting like I don't want a mate while we're on the island," he said. "It's working so far. None of the men are suspicious. Kyle will do what he can to continue making it sound like I'm not a threat. I won't be able to play hard in every challenge if I want to sell it, and I won't be able to go on every reward."

"Can you handle that, given the possessiveness?"

"I'll have to."

I tugged my hands free of his grasp and pulled my bra over my head. It had taken some wrestling to get it on before the game began, but those days were over. I'd already lost a little weight from the starvation. "Are you absolutely sure you want to do that? Because I'm not committing to you until you've convinced me you're certain, and we're not there yet."

His eyes flashed.

His hands landed on my bare waist. He was still naked, but I definitely didn't mind.

I got the feeling he wanted to walk me backward until he had me pinned to the wall, but he didn't.

"I'm not *wondering*, Chaos. You're mine, even when you're trying to push my buttons."

"I would never," I drawled.

His lips curved. "Right." He squeezed my hips lightly. "I'll convince you."

"I'll believe it when I see it."

"You'll see it."

I opened my mouth to keep the banter going, but before I could say anything else, he kissed me.

Slowly.

Softly.

Sweetly.

His tongue moved with mine, intimate and delicious.

"It's time," Jordan said.

"I have a plan to create more chaos, too," Rhett murmured, when he finally released my mouth.

My chest rose and fell quickly. "Now that's something I can get behind."

He chuckled, brushing his lips to mine one more time before he stepped back.

I followed Jordan into the hallway, Rhett close behind me, and found Kyle grinning knowingly.

"Wipe that smirk off your face," I grumbled at him, as we walked through the spa.

"Why? We're going to make this game our bitch."

"You do know that this plan requires you to lose again, right?" I checked.

"Running the game and saving good old Rhetti Spaghetti's life doesn't sound like losing."

I snorted. "Rhetti Spaghetti?"

"He loves pasta. Everyone knows that. I'm just the only one with enough guts to give him a nickname for it."

"For good reason," Rhett grunted.

The men shifted, and Rhett's arms went around me. His grip wasn't nearly as gentle as it had been the last time, which was satisfying. When I'd told him I wasn't going to break, he listened.

We took off, and the wind grew too loud to speak over.

Despite my lingering uncertainty, I felt good about our plan for the most part.

And even better about choosing Rhett.

· · ·

REID WAS GONE when we got back. I couldn't say I'd miss him.

The rain was still coming down, too.

It was kind of sad to go back to my "usual" sitting by myself and watching the waves roll, but that was the plan. So, I had no choice but to do it.

I started shivering when the sun disappeared behind some storm clouds partway through the day. Immediately, an illusion washed over me.

I was sitting on the beach, with my side pressed up against Rhett's.

His arm was around me, and the sun was shining down on us. Warmth flooded every cell of my body, and I leaned in closer to him.

We couldn't have a real conversation in the illusion—I wasn't free to do whatever I wanted inside it. Rhett had complete control.

But that didn't make it any less perfect. I was more than confident enough to let him take the helm, especially when his doing so meant giving me the illusion of feeling warm when I was shivering.

"If we weren't in this damn game, I'd put you on my lap and use my wings as an umbrella right now," he admitted.

I wanted to urge him to do it, just in the illusion, but had no way to say that.

So we remained where we were.

And even though it wasn't exactly what I wanted, it was enough to make my chest ache. I could do a lot worse than spending my life with a man thoughtful enough to do something about my shivering when it absolutely wasn't expected.

Somehow, when the illusion faded away, I was still warm.

I WAS EXHAUSTED when nighttime finally came around.

Rhett warmed me with his illusions every time I started shivering, but that didn't make it any easier to spend hours alone.

The rain finally stopped around dinnertime, and Harker started a fire despite the wood being wet. Magic was nice like that.

We all crowded around the fire.

I was squished between two guys I didn't really know—Travis and Chris—and Rhett's jaw was clenched, his attention solely on me.

Julian was watching him, almost suspiciously.

My mind flashed back to the first episode of the last season. Cameron had gotten rid of Julian immediately, because he was smart enough to put together their plan.

I'd have to tell Kyle or Rhett to get rid of him.

I focused on the fire until the rice was cooked through, then on my pitiful serving of it. There was some fish too, but it had been raining too hard for the guys to go out for long during most of the day, so I wasn't going to take that from them considering I'd had a massive breakfast.

I ate the rice slowly, not making eye contact with any of the men. They all avoided me too much to bother trying to befriend them.

They chatted about the lack of rain, some kind of fae sport that was popular, and the huge shark they'd seen while they were fishing the day before. The shark wasn't concerning to them—they were at the top of the food chain.

When I finished my rice, I looked up and found Rhett still watching me.

And Julian still watching him.

Shit.

I set my leaf down and stood up, not bothering to swat the wet sand off my ass and legs.

There was always wet sand on my ass and legs.

I missed the spa, badly.

Hell, I missed real life too.

"I'm going for a walk," I said.

Hopefully, Kyle could stop Rhett from coming after me.

I strode down the beach, and heard footsteps behind me.

My stomach clenched.

When I realized there were two sets, I relaxed a little.

Glancing at my sides, I found Kaden and Chris walking with me.

"So," one of them said.

I didn't reply.

The other cleared his throat. "We all had a discussion while you were gone," he said. "And we think it's unfair that we refused to let you sleep beside any of us when we knew you were too cold to sleep alone."

"You think?" I drawled.

"Yeah. We're sorry about that," Kaden admitted. "And we have a proposition for you."

"You do know that the term *proposition* has sexual connotation, right?"

His eyebrows lifted.

"An offer," Chris clarified. "We've all agreed to set up a rotation, and not to target whoever you sleep beside for that reason alone. I volunteered to go first."

They were more than a little late. Something told me that sleeping next to anyone but Rhett would be an instant no for him. That would create the kind of chaos I *didn't* want. The kind that would probably get him voted out of the game.

But I had to be careful about how I approached the offer. It would be too easy to imply that I wanted Rhett if I outright refused them. I had to give a valid reason.

"Did you also talk about the fact that I've been shivering from the cold nearly all day every day?" I asked, my voice even.

Neither of them responded.

I didn't think so.

My lack of enthusiasm about being the prize they were competing for had somehow managed to make them look at me like I wasn't a person at all. Let alone a woman they wanted to marry. They were focused on the game, and nothing but the game.

Or they just cared more about winning than about how I was feeling.

"Or the way I sit alone constantly, because you're all too chicken to talk to me? Or the differences between the kindnesses you've offered me and the ones you offered Molly during her season?"

More silence ensued.

Though I itched to bring up that Rhett was the only one who'd been kind to me, I didn't want to risk making him a target. So, I had to leave him out of it entirely.

"You don't get to pick and choose when you want to treat me well. I'm not participating in your shitty rotation."

With that, I picked up the pace and left them behind.

They watched me leave.

My chin lifted higher. Even if Rhett hadn't been there, playing for me, I wouldn't have gone along with their ridiculous plan. If they wanted to win me over, they should've started with a damn apology.

Then again, that also might not have worked.

I could hold a really great grudge.

I walked down the beach. Though the breeze made me cold, the lack of falling rain made up for that.

Taking a deep breath, I let it out slowly.

Everything was going to work out.

I just needed to make sure we got Julian out soon, and talk to Rhett about not staring at me. Even though I liked that he did.

And I had to somehow manage to act like I wasn't into him. Even though I was.

On top of surviving multiple more weeks on the island.

Yay.

I STAYED AWAY from the shelters until I was shivering badly, then finally headed back. I ran into Colt and Ian coming to look for me on my way back.

"You're freezing," Colt said, frowning.

"You talked to Chris and Kaden," I said flatly, walking right past them.

Both men caught me without a problem. Their long legs made that easy.

"We did, and we all feel bad," Ian admitted. "We're not selling ourselves as good potential mates."

"On that, we agree."

"Here." Colt draped his arm over my shoulder, but I ducked away as soon as its weight rested on me.

"Fuck off," I snapped. "Feeling bad doesn't give you the right to touch me."

He lifted his hands as if in surrender.

Ian did the same, but added, "We just want to keep you warm."

"I'm so used to shivering now, I don't even want to be warm."

It was obviously a lie, but the bitterness in my voice told them the truth.

"We'll have to work on a better apology," Colt said.

"I think you should all just fuck off the island so I can enjoy my life alone, actually," I said as we approached the shelter.

Rhett and Kyle were both sitting by the fire, leaning against a large log. Rhett's eyes narrowed when he saw me flanked by two men, and I wanted to smack the guy on the arm.

He was being too obvious.

"Good night," I snapped, striding right past all four men and whoever else was around as I went to mine and Rhett's usual spot in the shelter.

"Damn, she's pissed," one of the guys muttered. "Thought an apology would do it."

Kyle snorted. "I think Erin appreciates action more than words."

"When I tried to warm her up, it only pissed her off more," Colt protested.

"Grabbing someone without their permission isn't the good kind of action," Kyle said.

"You did that with Molly at least a dozen times," Colt pointed out.

"And I didn't win, did I?"

Silence was their response.

"How do we make it up to her, then?"

"I don't know. Let her call the shots or something," Kyle said. "We turned her down the last time she asked for help, so I think we're stuck waiting for her to ask again."

Someone groaned.

Someone else sighed.

"I knew the group snuggling was a shit idea."

"Then you should've volunteered to cuddle alone, bastard."

"What do we do about the sleeping arrangements?" someone else asked.

Rhett hadn't spoken. Hopefully it wasn't because he was too furious with me. I wasn't really sure what I could've done to make him mad, but he definitely hadn't seemed *happy*.

"She picked Rhett days ago," someone said glumly. "I think we have to ask him to keep doing it."

"Rhett?" someone asked.

He scoffed. "Fine."

The grumpiness in his response made my stomach tight with worry, even though I knew he was just playing the game.

I didn't want to get myself mated to someone who didn't want me. I *really* didn't want that.

Then again, it would be better to mate with someone who didn't want me, who I knew would treat me well, than the opposite.

So maybe it was fine.

And Rhett *did* want me. He'd said so himself. I was just... worried, I guess.

"She was shivering pretty badly," one of the guys said. "You should go now."

Rhett growled at them, but a minute later, lifted me up so he could lay beneath me in the shelter.

His eyes collided with mine, and the world twisted with another illusion.

We were on the warm beach again, watching the sunset. I was sitting on his lap, facing him, this time.

"You smell like Colt," he growled at me. "I want to kill the bastard for touching you."

The tightness in my stomach eased.

He pulled me to his chest, hugging me tightly to him. I could feel his grip loose in reality, and knew he was still playing the game, even if he wasn't absolutely terrific at it.

"I fucking hate seeing them touch you. Knowing I can't touch you. Not being able to sit down and talk like two normal people. This game is torture."

He continued, "Now, they're trying to convince you to like them. I don't know how to fucking handle it. Kyle's going to end up starting fights daily to keep the attention off my shitty self-control," he growled. "But the only way to get to the end if they realize I want you is to win all of the challenges, and some of these bastards are better at puzzles than I am."

There would be puzzle challenges, which meant Rhett probably couldn't win everything. Even if he was good at some kinds of puzzles, which I didn't know if he was, there would likely be at least one he couldn't win.

So, we couldn't just admit our relationship and hope for the best.

We had to play the game.

Despite the illusion filling my view, I tilted my face toward Rhett. His ear brushed my lips a moment later, and I whispered, "Julian is onto you. You have to stop glaring at everyone who's near me. Trust me."

He squeezed me tighter. "Of course I trust you. The plan Kyle put together requires a fuck ton of that trust. It just feels like it's going to be a damn miracle if I make it to the end of this thing."

He lowered his lips to my head and kissed the top of my wild hair. Maybe it was a good thing I hadn't chopped it. "We're going to have to start that chaos to get the attention off me."

"I'm listening."

My lips curved as he explained the idea him and Kyle had put together.

It was absolutely *vicious*.

I loved it.

eleven

ERIN

RHETT SILENTLY WOKE me up in the middle of the night, his eyes tired but warm as they moved over my face. There was a question in them.

I bit my lip but nodded, tilting my head to the side.

He lowered his mouth to my throat, and sucked lightly.

My grip on his chest tightened as wetness gathered between my thighs.

He sucked harder, and I bit back a moan.

It took everything I had not to rock against him, chasing my pleasure.

We had to keep it short and sweet. There were too many snoring bastards around to do anything else.

Rhett sucked harder, his hand catching my breast and grazing my hard nipple through my damp shirt. I'd need to take it off at a strategic time the next day.

After another moment, he pulled away, leaving me wet and horny as I caught my breath as silently as possible.

His illusion touched my mind.

"That was fucking sexy, and I'm still hard from earlier. The next time I get you alone, I'm not walking away until I've had you on my cock. Sleep well, Chaos."

His words and the peaceful image of us snuggling alone on the dry, warm beach lulled me back to sleep much faster than I expected.

Some part of me felt the light rain falling over us, washing away the scent of our desire and helping our plan.

Maybe the rain wasn't so bad after all.

THE NEXT MORNING, the plan started in full swing. The rain had stopped, so it felt like the sky was giving my evil plan its blessing.

The men were determined to start treating me better, which was exactly why the plan was starting when it was.

We had to take advantage of their stupidity, after all.

"Hey, Erin," Harker said cheerfully, as he and Kyle walked up to me together. "Want to take a walk with us to refill a few water bottles?"

I leaned back against the log behind me. Though the sun

was rising, and the island was finally starting to feel warm, I was still wearing my uncomfortably wet shirt.

Because between that and my hair, which I'd taken down from my ponytail, the hickey on my neck was totally hidden.

Ideally, I wanted to target Julian with my plan... but Harker would work if Julian didn't give me the opportunity.

Or maybe it would work out better if I went off with multiple men.

Hmm.

So many wicked options. I loved it.

"No," I said flatly. "I'm not walking off with both of you to give you a chance to try to befriend me if you're not willing to risk being seen talking to me alone."

I felt eyes on us.

Lots of eyes.

And there were probably even more ears. Everyone would know exactly where I stood on the issue of reverse-harem-style dating.

Kyle grinned and smacked Harker on the back. "I'll leave you to it, then." He strode off, putting Harker in a delightfully awkward situation.

Admit to being too scared of a target landing on him and turn me down... or go with me and embrace the target.

His expression grew slightly nervous, but he forced a smile. "Even better. Shall we?" He offered his elbow like an old-school gentleman.

Though the last thing I wanted to do was touch him, I reluctantly stood and took his elbow.

He led me down the jungle path that led to our water well. "It's nice that it stopped raining, right?" he asked, his voice coming off falsely cheerful. I didn't call him out for it.

"Yeah, finally," I agreed.

We chatted about the weather as we walked. It wasn't fun, but it could've been worse.

When we stopped at the well, he refilled the water bottles slowly, still going on about the rain.

I hated it as much as the next girl, but there was plenty more to talk about. He could've asked me about my job, my hobbies, or my family. Or *something*.

When he screwed the lid on the final water bottle, he offered me his elbow again. "Should we head back?"

I nodded, feigning hesitation.

He frowned, studying me.

"It's just that... you've been nice to me. No one's been nice to me since I got here," I confessed. Surging forward before he had time to react, I wrapped my arms around him and hugged him tightly. "Thank you so much. It's been really lonely here."

He slowly wrapped his arms around me and hugged me back. I bit back a grin at his obvious reluctance.

When I let go and stepped away, I took his elbow without waiting for him to offer it, and we headed back to camp together.

He brought up the weather again, and stumbled over the words a little. I felt kind of bad for catching him so off guard, but a girl had to do what she had to do to marry the man she wanted.

He'd signed up for the game. Now, he was going to play or be played.

NOT LONG AFTER we got back to camp, another guy asked me for a walk.

Colt.

I held his arm when he offered it, but didn't hug him. I needed to make sure everyone had a different story about their walk with me.

I went on a walk with Ev after that, and didn't touch him at all.

After walks with Chris and Ian, separately of course, Julian finally asked me to go with him.

The plan would kick off, then.

He didn't offer his elbow when we headed into the forest together, but I took it anyway.

Unlike some of the other guys, he asked about my life back home. Not wanting to share anything personal, I gave vague answers about my shitty job and the way I'd been sidelined because of my impending game show stint. He acted apologetic about that, but I didn't know if I believed him.

It didn't really matter if I did, because I wasn't risking him staying in the game to wreck Rhett's shot.

When he was ready to turn around and go back to the shelters, I put my plan into action.

To make Julian the target, I needed him to spend extra time in the jungle with me. And I needed him to smell like me even more than the other guys I'd touched.

So, I walked another minute with him before twisting my foot and crashing to the ground. Did it look like a realistic fall?

Probably not.

But I'd been genuine enough with the other guys that no one would believe him that I'd pretended to fall.

Hopefully.

"Are you okay?" Julian crouched beside me as I rolled to my ass, grimacing at the "pain" in my ankle.

"I'm fine," I said. "Just need to give this a minute before I put pressure on it."

He didn't look sold.

I rubbed it lightly, still grimacing.

A few minutes passed in awkward silence before he spoke again.

"I don't want to be out here too long," Julian said. "People will get suspicious."

"That's fair. Can you help me up?"

The look in his eyes told me he was finally starting to get suspicious of my plan and my *pain*.

But when I draped my arm over his shoulder, he stood up, dragging me to my feet with him.

"Thanks," I said, leaning heavily against him so my back pressed against some of his front.

My fingers brushed the back of his hair lightly, and he jerked away.

"You're fine," he said, stepping back.

I didn't have a problem staying upright, of course. I wasn't actually wounded.

"I'm going back to the shelter. See you there." His voice was clipped, and he strode away from me.

Perfect.

I crouched down, scooping some sand into my hand and lifting it to my mouth. Gently, I rubbed it over my lips. They needed to look a little swollen, to make people think I'd been kissed.

When they felt hot, I was satisfied, and headed back down the path until I found the branch of it that led to the beach.

It only took a minute to strip my shirt off and take a dunk in the water. Since the sun was shining for once, it was deliciously hot out, so my sports bra and shorts would dry quickly. My hair would take longer, so I tied it up in a ponytail after washing it. The ponytail was part of the plan, anyway.

After draping my shirt over a branch to dry, I strode back down the beach and headed to camp again, ready to watch the chaos unfold.

I saw a massive golden bird land down the beach while I was walking, and curiosity had me speeding up.

Molly, the pretty blonde girl from the first season, met me partway down the beach. Large but delicate golden wings hung off her back, reminding me that she'd mated with the fire guy, Cam.

She looked much more comfortable than I'd ever seen her on the show, and was wearing a pair of leggings and a t-shirt.

I raised my eyebrows when I saw her, careful not to greet her with a hug. I wanted it to be clear that I'd washed my scent clean. "How the hell did they talk you into coming back here?" I teased her.

She laughed. "They didn't. I packed a few things to make your trip a little more comfortable. Any way to stick it to the Society for dropping us here."

I smiled. "I can appreciate that. Thank you. Nice wings, by

the way." I gestured to her golden feathers. "How is it, being a fae?"

She shrugged. "Could be worse."

I snorted. "Could it, though?"

She laughed again, then handed me the backpack she'd brought. It probably wasn't much different than the one I'd packed for myself, but I wasn't going to tell her that when she'd made effort to be nice to me. And now that the sun was out, maybe I'd actually get some use out of everything.

We chatted a little about how much we both hated the island as we walked back to her mate. She said goodbye fairly soon, and left me before we ran into any of the men.

SURE ENOUGH, every eye was on me when I got back to camp. I hoped Julian hadn't said anything about my *fall*. Doing so would probably make other people suspicious of him, since I hadn't been anything but bluntly honest, but still. I didn't want anyone doubting me yet.

I felt the gazes lingering on my mouth—my lips still felt warm and swollen—as I grabbed a bottle of sunblock and took my seat beneath a tree again.

I was still only wearing my sports bra and shorts, with my wet hair tied up. The hickey on my neck was basically front and center. I hoped that was what they were staring at, rather than my tits.

The murmurs that broke out almost as soon as I sat down told me that the rumors and gossip were starting. I was too far to hear exactly what was being said, but I could imagine the possessive fae getting all riled up on the inside as they fought to maintain control on the outside.

I couldn't get involved in any of the conversations or push any more suspicion onto Julian than what already existed. So, I stayed where I was while the flurry of hushed conversation continued.

A boat showed up to take us to a challenge a few hours later.

Everyone kept their distance from me on the boat, especially Julian. I ended up standing in front of Rhett, who managed to look as bored and grumpy as usual.

Part of me worried he'd changed his mind, but I ignored that part. It wouldn't do me any good.

The boat ride was short, and then we were on an island, in front of a large table puzzle. It looked like a big maze, with a ball that would have to be navigated to the little dip in the center.

Shit.

Julian was smart.

He could win.

Then again, a puzzle like that wasn't just about being smart. It was also about coordination.

Which all of the fae guys probably had.

So... it was anyone's game.

I took my seat on the bench while Jordan explained the maze to everyone. The reward was a snorkeling trip that would bring me and the top two guys home late that night, after the voting was over.

When they began, I watched the game. Rhett was barely trying, which was expected.

But it also made me nervous, because it meant he was going to the vote. Which meant there was a chance he could be voted out.

It was slim, but... a chance was a chance.

I couldn't let my gaze linger on Rhett too long, just in case someone was watching, so I focused on Julian.

I was curious.

I'd seen the looks everyone was shooting him. He was totally the target. Winning the challenge would mean spending extra time with me, which was dangerous for him when he was already being targeted for that.

But losing would very likely mean getting voted out.

So either way, he was in trouble.

If I were him, I'd fight like hell to win the challenge. At least that would come with a few more days to stop being seen as a threat.

Sure enough, he finished first and stepped back, his hands in the air.

Jordan declared him the winner.

Ev finished soon after him.

Twenty minutes later, I was on a boat with both of them, feasting on shrimp tacos.

I didn't even like shrimp, but I was so hungry I didn't care.

When we were done eating, I leaned up against the boat's railing, watching the clear ocean on the horizon as we continued on. The wind blew through my ponytail, my hickey still on display though no one had mentioned it.

"So," Ev said, stepping up next to me.

Julian hadn't come anywhere near me since we left the jungle together. Which meant I needed to play the next few hours very carefully. It would be too easy for me to help Ev realize I wanted Julian out.

"So," I replied.

He chuckled. "That's a nice accessory you've got there."

I shot him a quick frown before looking back out at the water. Though I was pretty sure I knew what he was saying, I was going to make him spell it out. "What are you talking about?"

"The mark on your neck."

My forehead creased. "What?"

We didn't have a mirror on the island, so my cluelessness could totally be realistic.

Ev lifted an eyebrow. "You don't know?"

"Know what?"

He gestured to his own neck. "You've got a hickey."

My eyes flew open.

My face flushed.

I lifted a hand to the same side of my neck he'd gestured to.

"Other side."

My face flushed hotter, and I lowered my hands.

"Secrets can be hard to keep," he said. "Want to tell me the truth?"

I scowled at him, my face still warm as I looked away. "Screw off."

"Julian's been pretty quiet."

"Everyone's been pretty quiet," I shot back.

"Not everyone."

I clenched my jaw and said nothing.

"If you tell me the truth, I can try to save him," Ev said.

I didn't believe him.

And even if I did, I wouldn't have told him the actual truth. There was no way he'd believe me if I "opened up" anyway. He was looking for me to do something out of character, to prove to him that I was lying.

So, I stayed quiet.

He didn't bug me again, and when he changed the subject, I didn't participate much in the conversation.

It was a long, long date.

ERIN

HARKER WAS GONE when we got back.

I made a point to avoid Ev, and glared at him when he offered me a hand to help me out of the boat. Though I accepted the help, I released him as soon as I could and strode back to the shelter. As I went, I called in a flat voice, "I'm going to bed."

No one tried to stop me on my way there.

When Rhett joined me in the shelter, he held me casually, but lulled me to sleep with another mental image of us on a warm beach together. The things he murmured to me in the illusion told me he was struggling with smelling my scent on the other guys' skin, so I knew I needed to back off for a while if I could.

Acting like I'd been caught with Julian required keeping to myself more the next few days, so I did exactly that. It calmed Rhett's possessiveness down, too.

Julian won the next challenge as well. It was a different kind of puzzle, so Ev went home in the next vote.

When Kyle won the challenge after that, he got to choose two guys to go with us. He picked both Rhett and Travis for our outing to a little bar nearby. Having Travis there meant Rhett and I couldn't talk freely or spend any real time together, which was shitty.

But Julian was gone when we got back after the vote.

With him out, the biggest threat to Rhett's game was gone, so I finally relaxed for a few days.

Of course, *relaxing* didn't mean I could spend any more time with Rhett. But it wasn't raining anymore, so I tried to enjoy it.

ON THE MORNING of day 17, I woke up early. Rhett was still sleeping, so I slid off his chest quietly and padded out to the beach.

I walked along the sand alone, watching the sunrise as I went. It was windy, which didn't seem like a great sign as far as the weather went, but I tried not to worry about that.

There were bigger things to deal with.

We were only a little over halfway through the game.

It felt like I'd survived a lifetime on the beach. I wasn't sure how I was going to make it another thirteen days, but I also wasn't sure what it would be like to go back to reality anymore.

I itched to sit down with Rhett and have a conversation about what life would actually look like if I chose him in the end like we were planning. I barely knew the guy. And while I did like him, forever was a lot to promise someone.

Granted, I hadn't actually *promised* anything.

I hadn't even completely agreed to go along with his plan.

Maybe I needed to rethink that.

Thunder rumbled overhead, and I grimaced. Though the sun was rising, I was well aware of how quickly storm clouds could come in and change everything.

I forced myself to consider the main reason I was working with Rhett.

The reason I'd attempted creating chaos in the game.

Because I didn't want to land in an abusive relationship. And Rhett was a lot of things, but he wasn't an abuser. He was patient. Laid-back, even.

I would be safe with him, and that was what I wanted.

But... what if I wanted more, too?

According to him, fae couldn't abuse their mates. Which meant that every man on the island could actually be a potential mate for me.

And as much as I liked Rhett, he hadn't really shown the dominance I wanted in a guy. I didn't want someone cruel, but I didn't want someone too soft, either. I would walk all over one of the *nice guy* types.

Not that Rhett was really a *nice guy*.

I just...

I didn't know.

It was a big decision. A really big decision.

Not one I wanted to make while I was uncertain, that was for damn sure.

THE WIND PICKED up as the day continued.

The sky darkened too, but no rain fell.

I held my ponytail back as the boat carried us away from our island and into the middle of a rainstorm over the island I recognized from the first day of *Survival*.

Thankfully, the showrunners had set up a large, permanent canopy. It was made of metal, and didn't move even slightly in the heavy wind, which made me think they'd drilled it into the ground or something.

I sure as hell wasn't complaining.

All of us gathered beneath the canopy as Jordan announced a different kind of contest. The guys seemed to know what he was talking about when he called it the "care package challenge" and said everyone would win that day.

When they all headed into the pouring rain to look for their care packages, I asked him for more details.

"They did this challenge in the first season," he explained. "All of the guys packed a bag with three things in it as well as an asset folder. The items could be things for their comfort or your comfort. The asset folder has pictures and information about their life back home. Each of them will get a few minutes to show you the items and explain the folders' contents to you."

Oh.

That was actually kind of helpful.

I wouldn't admit it aloud, of course. But it was.

I'd just been thinking about how I would choose someone without knowing anything about what my life with them would look like. And I'd just been wondering if I really wanted to put all my eggs in Rhett's basket. Figuratively, of course.

Maybe the care package thing would help me decide.

"Last season, I think there was an extra care package or something to determine the winner," Jordan added. "But they did it later in the season, and Molly didn't have as many comfort items as you do, so they nixed that this time. The first guy back is the one who gets extra time with you. The other bastards will sit out in the rain a little longer."

I felt bad for them, but they had signed up to play.

Except Rhett.

I couldn't help but wonder if someone else had packed stuff

for him, or if he just wasn't going to have anything in his bag at all.

We didn't have to wait long for the first guy to return. There were seven men left in the game, though, so it was going to take a while to go through all the information they all brought.

Ian was back through the trees quickly, flashing me a grin as he sat down next to me and shook water from his hair. I didn't bother closing my eyes when he did, but wiped my face off afterward.

That was annoying.

I could check one guy off the list.

It was probably petty to remove him from the standings just because he shook water all over me like a dog, but I was pretty okay with that level of pettiness.

"Sorry about Julian," Ian said, unzipping the bag. It was waterproof, so everything inside had been protected.

I was supposed to be upset Julian was gone.

Oops.

I scowled, and Ian flashed me an apologetic look. "It's just the game," he said. "It irks at a fae's possessiveness to know someone was comfortable enough with you to kiss you like that, even though we know logically that you just liked him."

He pulled the first item from his bag. It was a blanket.

His expression was sheepish. "Here's a third blanket for you. Won't do much good if it starts raining again, but still."

"Thanks."

The second two items were candy. Gummy candy, in sets that were the shape of burgers, hot dogs, pizza, and other snack foods.

"I wanted to bring the real thing, but this is as close as I could get," he teased, handing me the treats.

The idea was silly, but clever. My smile in response was genuine. "Thank you."

"Any time." He winked. "Now, I've got an asset folder." He waved a manilla folder before he opened it up. "Pictures of my house are on top. My family beneath. My job's on the bottom."

I took the thick cardstock pages of photos that he'd included. His house looked like a mansion in the forest—not exactly shabby.

His family consisted just of him and his parents, but they looked nice, and there was a picture of their house too. It was a few miles down the road from his, according to the page.

The photos of his job showed him in a science lab, shooting the camera a thumbs up as he made faces or grinned at different places in the room.

"You're a scientist?" I asked, surprised.

"Yep. I've been working with a few other fae to try to figure out how to turn humans into compatible mates. We haven't had any success yet," he explained. "But we invented a few different medications for humans in the process."

Hot damn, he was smart.

"So, if we mated..." I trailed off, wanting to hear his explanation.

"You could do whatever you want," he said simply. "I spend a lot of time at the lab, so you'd be pretty much free to your own devices. Get a job, go to school, start making pottery. I don't particularly care."

Ah.

Well, that was better than I'd hoped before I ended up on the show. But I couldn't say it was exactly what I wanted.

Not that I really knew what I wanted.

He told me a story about his lab, and I listened half-heartedly as my mind continued moving.

I had to figure out what I did want, so *not* wanting to live like he'd offered was a good place to start.

What didn't I like about the offer?

It took me a few minutes to wrestle my feelings enough to figure it out.

Freedom would be nice, but when it came down to it, I didn't *only* want to be free. Not if I was going to be mated. If I was tying my life to someone's, I didn't want to wonder where he was or what he was doing. I didn't want to be at the bottom of his priority list. I wanted us to be a team, to do things together.

So, I didn't want Ian because of the life he wanted to live.

That was a much fairer reason not to choose him than the way he'd shaken water all over me like a dog, too.

WHEN IAN'S time was finally up, Kyle sat down with me and set his backpack on his lap. He handed me his folder, the sweatshirt and hat he'd packed for me, and the box of Twinkies.

We both ate one, neither of us bringing up our plan to get Rhett to the end as I flipped through his folder like I'd consider him.

We knew I wouldn't, though.

After him, I talked to Chris and Travis. Chris seemed nice, and I didn't dislike anything he said to me. Travis seemed pretty boring.

But nothing either of them said made me think they were who I wanted to mate with.

Colt and Kaden took their turns after Travis. I liked both of them and what they offered, and both of them were fairly easy to talk to. That was nice. I'd chatted with them before, but watching them talk about their lives was different. Neither of them said anything that made me think I'd hate living with them, either.

By the time Rhett finally sat down in front of me, I had a gigantic pile of treats off to my side, a few new blankets, and a large fishing hat.

Colt liked to fish outside the game, hence the hat.

"Did you really pack that?" I asked Rhett, glancing at the bag.

The other guys were watching us, so we needed to seem as neutral toward each other as usual.

"Nope." Rhett unrolled the top of the waterproof bag. "Christina probably did it."

The Society's leader herself actually packed Rhett's bag? That was kind of intense.

There was a thick card on the top, and he handed it over to me as he reached into the bag.

I read the contents quickly.

> Erin,
> Rhett didn't pack a bag, so I picked up a few of the comfort items you should've bargained for before the game started ;) He's like a son to me, so it's the least I could do.
> You're over halfway done!
> Love,
> Christina
> P.S. I'm not allowed to pick sides, but I'm sure whoever you choose will be a perfect mate.

You'll have to stop by for dinner with Molly and the mates when it's over!

I looked up when Rhett whistled.

"You're going to like this."

My eyes widened when I saw a shiny red jacket. It looked waterproof.

When I reached over and felt the sleeves, I found it even more rubbery than I expected.

I ripped it from his hands immediately.

If I hadn't been watching Rhett's expression, I would've missed his smile.

The rain jacket was oversized, and had a gigantic hood too.

It was perfect.

I hugged it to my chest.

I officially loved Christina.

There were a pair of rain boots beneath it.

She was legitimately my new favorite person.

"Can I mate with Christina?" I checked.

He snorted and handed me his folder. "Charlie would kill you if you tried to steal his woman."

I opened it up, still hugging my new boots as I did so. "Where do you live?"

Even as the question came out, I saw pictures of a gorgeous, coastal home planted right on a beach.

Damn, it was beautiful.

My gaze lingered on the photos of the view from the balcony, where I would be able to watch the ocean at any time. "It's stunning."

"Cameron and Molly live a few doors down from me," he said. "Christina and her husband Charlie do too, in the opposite direction."

As much as I didn't like the island, I did love the view. A beach house was tempting.

I itched to ask him to tell me more about what being mated to him would be like, but if he did so, everyone would realize he wasn't just being dragged along anymore.

So I didn't.

Beneath the house pictures, I found photos of him with Cameron and a nice-looking older couple. The label above it said they were Christina and Charlie Cassette, the leaders of fae Society.

A picture of him with his parents was beside it.

And beneath those, there was a sheet that had pictures of him guarding in the *Bachelorette* game show, as well as in *Survival.*

I wanted to ask what he'd do about work if we mated, too, but couldn't bring that up either.

Not when we had secrets to keep and a game to play.

So, I just closed the folder and set it on top of the stack of others I'd been given.

"You have a nice house. Too bad you're not interested in winning," I finally said.

He gave a noncommittal grunt, and our time was over.

I didn't hesitate to put on my new coat and boots. I was already soaked, but I wasn't about to get any wetter when there was another option.

So, I zipped myself up and followed Rhett and the others back to the boat.

I wasn't sure who was going to get voted out that night, but I figured it was probably a good thing I didn't. Because I had no idea who I was rooting for anymore.

thirteen

RHETT

ERIN STARTED DISTANCING herself from me more than usual after the care package challenge. I wasn't sure why, but it seemed likely that someone else had said something to make her think they'd be a better mate.

Which made me see fucking red.

I couldn't admit that, though.

So when the other guys went for a walk and Erin went with them, I leaned over to Kyle and said, "I need to talk to her."

He and I were sitting in front of our dead firepit while the rain poured down.

He raised his eyebrows. "That's too risky, Rhetti."

"She's uncertain. I need to calm her fears. One of the other bastards might've said something to make her want them."

"I was there the whole time. She didn't seem interested in any of them."

"I can't take that risk."

"You can and will," he said bluntly. "Our only goal is to get you to the end."

"She has to choose me when we get there," I growled.

"She will."

My flat look told him how much I believed him.

Kyle smacked me on the thigh. "Listen, my man. You can get to the end safely, or you can risk everything to make sure you and Erin are on the same page. Cameron went with the first option, and it worked for him. You can try to talk to her if you want, but there's no guarantee it'll work out. And a little uncertainty seems better to me than risking your entire game—and life—for a conversation.

I clenched my jaw.

Kyle changed his approach. "Her conversations went the smoothest with Kaden and Colt. She seemed to like Kade the most. Why don't we just target one of them tonight? I can get Travis and Chris to vote with us if I approach it right."

We'd been planning to vote with Chris, Ian, and Colt to get rid of Travis that night. He didn't particularly trust Kyle despite getting to the end with him in the first season, so Kyle wanted him out.

But, if Erin was even slightly interested in Kaden, we needed to get rid of him.

Followed by Colt.

As soon as possible.

So, I jerked my head in a nod. "Kaden goes home."

"I'll make it happen," Kyle agreed. "For the love of fae, don't do anything stupid. I can't drag your ass to the end if you make yourself a target."

As frustrating as it was, he was right.

I'd have to figure out another way to make Erin more confident in me. One that didn't risk my place in the game.

Gritting my teeth, I remained where I was and put together a plan while Kyle headed into the jungle to talk to some of the guys.

THE VOTE WENT DOWN EXACTLY as we planned—me, Kyle, Travis, and Chris against the other three—and Kaden went home.

Kyle chatted with Erin on his way back to the shelters, his hands in his pockets while hers were tucked in her raincoat. We were still getting poured on, and there was an assload of wind.

She stayed quiet during the walk, and called it a night as soon as we were there. Everyone else did too.

. . .

HER COAT SQUEALED every time she moved on top of me, so both of us stayed extremely still as everyone started going to sleep. Her position was a little stiffer than usual, and I itched to have her bare skin touching me instead of the rubber jacket. But, I was just glad she was there.

As soon as she was settled, I closed my eyes and started the illusion I'd been planning. Like usual, she tensed against me before she relaxed again.

Instead of sitting on the Survival island like usual, we stared up at my house.

It wasn't as fancy as many of the fae's homes—I didn't want a mansion—but I kept up with everything and updated it when I needed to.

I didn't know how she'd really react to seeing my house, so I didn't impose much on her in the illusion. It would feel more realistic for her to be along for the ride than to be reacting incorrectly.

The scent of saltwater was heavy in the air, and we could hear the waves rolling to the shore. I slipped my hand in hers and led her up to the doorstep. I wanted to scoop her off her feet and carry her myself, but once again, didn't want to put her off.

Not just because of the illusion, but because I was worried she'd find me overbearing.

So, we walked up to the door. She opened it, and my hands found her hips as she stepped inside.

"Welcome home," I murmured to her, as she took everything in. Her steps were long and her eyes bright while I led her through the house, showing her everything.

The tour landed in my room.

Our room.

I couldn't risk turning her on too much while there were other men around us, so I only allowed myself to kiss her neck lightly. "I'll make you happy here, if you let me," I said simply.

I wanted to tell her that I'd fuck her on every surface in the house.

That I'd make love to her pressed against a window, so she could watch the waves while she came undone on my cock.

That we'd talk while we cooked together, decide which of the Society's jobs to work and reject together, and just overall enjoy life together.

But without a conversation, I didn't know where her mind was at.

So, I had to be careful about the overbearing thing. Being too much was a good way to chase her into someone else's arms.

We sat down on a porch swing that had never been used and watched the waves together until her eyelids grew heavy and she fell asleep in my arms, both in the illusion and in real life.

It wasn't the conversation I wanted to have, but it would have to do.

fourteen

ERIN

I WOKE up early again the next day and went out to walk along the beach through the sunrise like I had the day before.

It was a good way to start a day.

Though it was still drizzling, it had eased up enough to be peaceful. My coat helped with that too.

Biting my lip, I paused after a particularly rough wave and stared out at the horizon.

It was beautiful, but that wasn't on my mind.

Rhett was.

He was...

Well, I didn't know exactly.

We hadn't gotten to spend a lot of time together. He was a

lot rougher when we first met. There'd been a quiet intensity about him that lured me in.

Now, he just seemed... gentle.

Too gentle.

And quiet.

And easy-going.

None of which were bad things. They just weren't who I thought he was, which made me doubt everything.

On top of that, I didn't want a quiet and easy-going life. Yeah, I wanted safety, but not at the cost of enjoying myself.

Which was a conundrum.

Maybe I just had bad taste in men, because what woman wouldn't want a polite, nice guy?

It was no wonder fate made me compatible with the fae. I was probably better off with Kyle than Rhett. At least with Kyle, there would be arguments.

And speak of the devil...

Kyle came strolling up to me, ignoring the rain altogether. "Hey."

"Hi."

"You look thinky," he said, gesturing to my face.

"It's called having a brain."

He grinned. "Is it?"

I rolled my eyes at him, and he tucked his hands in the pockets of his shorts. The bastard was lucky he was so big, or he would've been freezing.

Like I would've been, without my new favorite possessions. My coat and boots would be my best friends for the rest of my life, at the rate we were going.

"Rhett thinks you're upset about something," Kyle said.

I glanced over my shoulder to make sure we were alone.

"Everyone else was still asleep when I walked away, and the jungle is too far from us for anyone hiding there to hear us. We're good," he added.

"I'm not upset," I said, refocusing on the water. "Just... uncertain, I guess."

"About what?"

I hesitated.

"You're sexually attracted to me, aren't you?" he drawled.

I smacked him on the arm. "Shut up."

He grinned.

"I don't know him very well," I finally said. "Which is fine. I don't need to know everything about him. But I need to know what his personality's like before I marry him, you know? That shit's permanent."

Kyle made a noise of agreement. "It is."

"And..."

"And what part of his personality are you uncertain about?"

"He's just been acting... nice. And laid-back," I said.

Kyle blinked.

"I know it sounds ridiculous," I added hastily. "Those aren't bad characteristics. It's just that when we were around each other at first, he was more intense. And rougher. Now, he's so calm in all the illusions he sends me. Sometimes, calm is good. But it gets boring, you know? I want him to know what he wants, and assert himself. Not just be nice."

Kyle blinked again. "I don't know anyone who would call Rhett *nice*."

My forehead creased. "You don't?"

"No. He does the Society's dirty work more often than not. Doesn't exactly leave him room for kindness."

"Oh."

"Yeah. If he's being too nice, he's probably just trying not to scare you off."

That made me feel better.

A lot better.

If he was trying not to scare me off, that would explain his over-politeness. And the blandness I'd started to feel sometimes in his illusions.

"Since I can't talk to him, can you tell him to stop being so nice?"

Kyle sighed. "Alright. You'll owe me, though."

"What do you want?"

"A kiss." He tapped his lips.

I narrowed my eyes at him, and he grinned again.

"I'm teasing. Just put in a good word for me with the next girl if you get to meet her."

"Deal."

We headed back toward the shelters, and my thoughts moved a bit faster.

I didn't know what Rhett would do when Kyle talked to him, but I was kind of excited to find out.

THAT DAY PASSED JUST like all the others, and I was relieved when it was finally time to call it a night. I got cozy next to Rhett as if I *didn't* want to fuck him, like always.

He barely touched me, which was also our usual.

I remained awake, tense and waiting for him to do something while everyone around us fell asleep one by one.

It was still sprinkling a little, but that was the last thing on my mind.

When I finally started to drift off, Rhett's hand found my ass.

My eyes opened.

In a smooth motion, he swept me out of the shelter and carried me into the jungle. His feet were silent, and I clung to his neck, my heart beating wildly against his chest.

Maybe he wasn't too nice after all.

I didn't say a word as he hauled me deeper into the jungle, finally stopping when we reached the well. He set me down on the rough brick ledge of it, and I barely noticed that some parts were sharp against my ass.

As soon as I was sitting, he took my face between his gigantic hands and looked me square in the eyes. "We're playing a game, Chaos."

"I know that."

"A game that requires me to hide everything I am and feel," he continued, his gaze piercing. "I want to touch you, but I can't. I want to hold you, kiss you, fuck you—but I can't. I have to play the game. That doesn't mean I don't want you. It means I have to keep the illusions bland, because if I let myself say and do what I want, we're both going to give ourselves away and ruin our game in the process."

That... made sense.

I should've put it together myself, actually.

I guess insecurity had been in the driver's seat. Given the situation, the insecurity did seem reasonable, though.

"There are only a few votes left," Rhett said. "Eight more days, then we won't have to pretend anymore. I need you to make it through them without doubting me, Chaos. What can I do to make that easier for you?"

"I don't know," I admitted. "But I'll survive. I'll figure it out."

"Alright." Rhett started releasing my face, but paused.

And after a moment—a short beat of hesitation—he tilted his head down and brushed his lips against mine.

The kiss was soft.

Too soft.

I lifted my hands to his hair and buried them in the strands, pulling him down closer as I parted my lips.

His tongue met mine without pause, stroking slowly.

Intimately.

My legs wrapped around his waist, pulling him closer. I wanted more—*needed* more.

Rhett tilted my head back, deepening the kiss. His hands left my face, finding the zipper at the top of my raincoat. I leaned back just enough that he could pull it down and peel it off my body while he kissed me.

My boots were still back at camp, so with the jacket gone, all I had on was my bra and shorts.

The rain was still falling, but it didn't feel cold anymore.

Rhett's hands were rough as they slid over my bare hips, finding the hem of my sports bra. I expected him to tease my breasts through the fabric after the last time we'd been together, but he didn't bother.

He hooked his fingers beneath the hem, released my mouth for a moment, and peeled it over my head.

A growl vibrated his chest when he looked down at my bare breasts, nipples hard as rain fell over my skin.

The rain wasn't miserable anymore.

It was kind of hot.

"You're fucking gorgeous," he rumbled, taking my breasts and slowly dragging his thumbs over my nipples.

My hips moved a little, and the bite of the rough brick against my backside only made me want him more.

"Are you going to let me walk away without taking what you want again?" I asked, arching my back a little to put more of my tits in his hands.

He squeezed them in response, making me suck in a breath.

"I should," he said, his hot eyes on my breasts. "I should take you back to camp before someone realizes we're gone."

"They're all asleep," I said, reaching for his cock. His shorts didn't hide his erection even a little.

I dragged my hand down the length of him.

He stepped closer, giving me better access. "It's a risk, Chaos."

"Live a little, Rhetti." I tossed Kyle's nickname for him out there, just to see how he reacted. "Accept your dominance. Take what you want. I'll stop you if it's too much."

He released my breasts.

I opened my mouth to protest, but the words didn't escape, because he kneeled between my thighs.

His fingers hooked in the waistband of my shorts, and he tugged them down my thighs and calves, dropping the fabric on the dirt. With his hands on the insides of my knees, he opened my legs wide.

He made a sound of appreciation. "Already slick for me, Chaos?"

"Always."

He dragged a hand up my thigh and slowly traced a circle around my clit, making me shudder. "I want to take my time with you, but I shouldn't."

"Then don't."

His eyes lifted to mine, holding my gaze as he leaned in and dragged his tongue in the same shape he'd just made with his finger.

I gasped at the sensations.

It had been years since I'd had sex—and I'd been younger then. The guys weren't experienced. No one had ever gone down on me before.

His chest rumbled. "You taste just as good as you smell." He ran his tongue over me again, slow and light. "How does that feel?"

"So good." I buried one hand in his hair as I arched my hips, opening wider for him. "Keep going."

"You want more?"

"*Yes.*"

He licked me again, slower, but with more pressure.

Holy shit.

Holy *shit.*

He kept going.

And going.

And going.

Until I was crying into the jungle, yanking on his hair as the pleasure rolled from my head to my toes.

Despite my release, I still wanted more.

Needed more.

I should've been quieter, but I was too lost to my lust to care.

It didn't take a rocket scientist to know he was too.

"Rhett," I said, pushing his face away from my drenched center. "I need you inside me."

He didn't hesitate for a moment, standing and pushing his shorts to the ground.

I wrapped my fingers around his erection, but he pulled me off the brick wall of the well and put me back on my feet. My bare chest met his, and the feel of it was everything.

He walked me backward until my shoulder blades met a tree, then lifted one of my thighs as he tugged my hand off his cock. I sucked in a breath when he lined the tip up against my opening.

Our eyes were locked together.

But then a tree branch snapped in the jungle behind us.

Rhett moved so fast, it made me dizzy.

He put me behind him, my body completely concealed from the intruder with his. I tried to look over his shoulder, but he was too damn big.

I didn't hear the footsteps, but Rhett's noise of warning told me someone was coming. "Don't take another step."

His voice was so ferocious, *I* definitely wouldn't have risked going against his order.

"How long have you been together?" another male voice asked.

The voice was tight, but I recognized it immediately.

Colt.

Shit.

I squeezed my eyes shut.

Colt was better than Travis, at least. Travis would've gone back to camp and told everyone. Colt might do exactly that—but he could be a little more careful about it.

Hopefully.

"Since the spa," Rhett gritted out.

He didn't tell Colt we hadn't actually fucked. That wasn't his business, and it wasn't necessary information.

"You should've told me," Colt finally said, his voice nearly as low as Rhett's.

"Why? You want a mate as badly as any of these other bastards."

Colt let out a humorless laugh. "And you don't?"

"No. I don't want *a mate*," Rhett growled.

My chest tightened.

"I want *Erin*," he said.

The tightness vanished immediately.

That was actually kind of romantic. Or really romantic.

"Go back to camp," Rhett said. Though it wasn't an order, it kind of was. "If you're going to tell the others, tell them. There's no point in wasting time with any more bullshit. Erin is mine."

"Not if you don't make it to the end," Colt growled back.

"Fuck off," Rhett snarled.

I heard footsteps as the other man walked away, but Rhett didn't let go immediately.

"We need to wash off in the ocean and get back fast," I said, pushing on his back as I stepped away. Though he released me, he didn't go far.

"There's no reason to hurry. Whether or not he tells them, we won't get back in time to stop anyone from believing him."

Panic swelled in my chest. "We have to, Rhett. I'm not going to mate with one of them if you get voted out. I can't. I—"

He caught my waist with one hand, and put the other on the center of my chest. I clutched his arm, holding tightly. "Do you trust me, Chaos?"

I did.

Probably.

Mostly.

Enough to nod, at least.

"Then believe that Colt won't tell anyone. He won't make himself the only reason I'm removed from the game he knows I'll win. Not when losing will mean fading entirely for me."

"That's not how this game is supposed to work," I whispered.

"It's not," he agreed. "But it will."

"You're insane."

His lips curved upward slightly. It was another one of those quick, sexy as hell smiles. The ones he reserved just for me. "Maybe."

"Definitely." I pushed away from him. "Not all of the guys will work with him to keep you in the game."

"No. Travis and Ian would fight like hell to get rid of me if they knew. And if the two of them wanted me out, Colt would vote with them, and get someone else on his side. He respects me, but we're not friends."

"That's risky," I said, shaking my head. "Too risky. We need to wash up and go back. We need—"

"We need to keep our distance from each other like we were doing," Rhett said. "I'll do what I can to win the rest of the challenges, in case Colt decides to speak up. We'll stay away from each other outside of sleeping, just to be safe. There are only a few days left. We can do this."

I nodded, even though I wasn't sure I believed him. Not entirely, at least.

And while I didn't believe him completely, I hoped like hell that he was right.

Because I couldn't mate with any of the other guys. Not anymore. Not when I wanted Rhett the way I did.

ERIN

JUST LIKE HE PROMISED, Rhett won the next challenge. The reward was another boat ride. Because Kyle went with us, I spent the whole trip curled against Rhett's side. We didn't talk much—the wind was too loud to have a real conversation.

Ian was gone when we got back from our reward.

The air on the island seemed more tense, but the rain stopped, at least.

Though I caught Colt glaring at me a few times, I tried not to let it get to my head.

THREE UNCOMFORTABLE DAYS LATER, Rhett won the next challenge too. Kyle took second, so the three of us were off together again.

The reward was a flight to a beautiful lookout point at the top of a mountain, where we had a picnic dinner. After we were done eating, Kyle made up an excuse about going for a walk and made himself scarce, leaving me alone with Rhett.

"So," Rhett said, as I stared out at the islands and ocean on the horizon.

"So."

He set his hand on my thigh, and I couldn't help but look at him.

"I want to kiss you," he said. "But you seem mad at me."

I scowled. "I'm not mad. I'm just…"

Terrified you'll lose the next challenge.

Worried I'm going to get stuck with Colt, who clearly hates me.

Afraid I'll end up married to Kyle when I want you.

"Nervous," I finally said.

Rhett's expression told me he didn't believe me, but he didn't say anything to argue.

Instead, he lifted me off the picnic blanket and set me on his lap, so I was straddling him.

My body warmed when I felt his erection against me. "There are cameras," I said.

"Everyone behind them knows exactly who you belong to." He slid a hand over my hip. "They'll delete the footage."

"Rhett," I warned, though whatever I'd been about to say disappeared from my mind when his hand slid over my face, tucking a few strands of hair behind my ear.

"I just want to kiss you, Chaos," he murmured. "Nothing else."

My throat swelled. "What if you lose?"

"I won't lose."

I was still scared.

But when Rhett's lips met mine, he wiped that fear away until all that was left was desire.

We made out on the mountain until it was time to go back to the game, never letting it go further than that.

But damn, I wanted more.

WHEN WE ARRIVED on the island again, there were no pleasantries.

No polite greetings.

No hellos.

I noticed immediately that Colt was gone.

Travis stormed toward us, and Rhett tucked me behind his back, where I was safe.

When Travis shoved him, Rhett moved me behind Kyle in one smooth motion, without turning to face me.

"What the fuck, man?" Travis snarled. "You show up and tell us you're not playing the game, then go behind our backs and screw the woman we're all fighting for?"

Colt must've told them about walking in on us when they were voting him out.

Lovely.

"I've played in the challenges the same way you have," Rhett said, his voice surprisingly calm.

"Not by choice!"

"I have wings. I could've left the island the moment I realized what Christina planned. I could've left the game. I chose to stay, which means I chose to play. It's not my fault you didn't put the facts together," Rhett said.

Travis tried to shove him again.

Rhett caught his wrists. "Think very carefully about your next actions. I'm not allowed to kill you, but I can make your life very, very painful."

Travis glowered at Rhett, but Rhett didn't shrink. He simply released Travis's hands and stood his ground.

Whatever lingering doubt I'd had about whether or not Rhett was the kind of guy I should marry vanished entirely. Travis had literally attacked him, and he didn't lose his temper, flinch, or even really react except to stop the confrontation,

He was steady.

At ease.

Confident.

It was as sexy as it was reassuring.

"What's going on, exactly?" Kyle asked.

We'd told him about Colt catching us, so he was just asking so he could play along.

If and when Rhett won, Kyle would have to come back to the island to play again. So, he needed to maintain a relationship with the other guys as much as possible.

"Colt found them screwing a few days ago," Travis snarled back. "He told us at the council."

"How sure are you that it's true?" Kyle countered.

"He didn't deny it." Travis tossed a hand toward Rhett. "Neither did she."

Shit.

Guess we should've protested.

"It's true," Rhett said, leveling his gaze with Kyle's. "Erin is mine."

The simple declaration made me warm all over.

"You'd better hope you win the next challenge, then," Kyle retorted.

"I will." Rhett didn't hesitate.

There was no room for uncertainty.

Because if he *didn't* win…

Well, I wasn't going to consider that.

He had to win.

Or I'd have to mate with Kyle.

RHETT TOOK my hand and led me back to the shelter we'd always slept in. It had grown emptier over the weeks, and Colt and Travis had been the only ones who slept in it with us anymore.

Considering Colt was gone and Travis had flipped out, it seemed safe to say we'd be sleeping in it alone.

"Sorry," I whispered. "I should've claimed Colt was lying."

"I should've too," Rhett admitted. "Lying doesn't come naturally to me."

"That's a good thing."

"Anywhere but here, it is."

Rhett pulled me down to the shelter's uneven base again and wrapped me in his arms. For the first time ever, I let myself hug him the way I wanted to, my fingertips digging into his skin lightly and my leg draped over his cock.

It grew and hardened beneath me, and my lips curved upward slightly. "How much privacy do we have in here?"

His arms tightened around me. "Not enough for what I want to do to you."

Sighing, I nodded against his chest and closed my eyes. "I know this isn't what you wanted, but I'm glad you're here."

"I wouldn't trade it for anything." His voice was quiet, but made my throat thicken anyway.

I stayed in his arms for a long time, but eventually, sleep took over.

THE NEXT FEW days were spent tucked against Rhett's side. Though there were things we needed to discuss, neither of us wanted to have those tense conversations while Travis was glaring at us so heatedly.

I did ask Rhett if we needed to worry about Travis using his magic on me, considering he could basically force me to do things I didn't want to do. His reply that Travis wasn't smart, but was too smart to risk *that*, put me at ease.

So, we sat.

And snuggled.

It was actually kind of nice.

Unlike Travis, Chris didn't glare at all. I actually heard him murmur a *congrats* to Rhett in passing, when Travis wasn't around.

Kyle tried to lighten the mood with jokes, teasing everyone that Rhett had "outsmarted us", but it didn't work.

Travis was too furious.

. . .

WHEN THE FINAL CHALLENGE ARRIVED,

my stomach hurt so badly, I worried I might throw up.

Rhett held me to his chest while the boat sped to the island, but it didn't calm my nerves.

Not when I knew what was at stake.

I took my seat on the bench when we reached the island, and heard Travis grumble, "It's the same stupid puzzle from the last challenge of last season."

"I hope they at least replaced Molly with Erin," Kyle said with a snort.

My forehead creased, and I looked over all of them.

None of the remaining four men were good at puzzles. Kyle was absolute shit with them, and Travis was too. But Rhett and Chris?

They were probably equal. Not great, and not terrible.

Jordan had the men all take their places in front of large platforms. I assumed they would be building the puzzle on those.

When he announced the start of the challenge, the men immediately began.

Kyle started sorting the pieces. Rhett did too.

Travis tried them randomly, his expression growing more frustrated with every one he got wrong.

Chris's tactic was a mixture of sorting and testing.

"What were they saying about the puzzle?" I whispered to Jordan, knowing he wasn't allowed to give me much information but would tell me what he could.

"The final puzzle last season formed a large statue of Molly," Jordan murmured back.

So the guys thought this one was of me.

I wrinkled my nose at the idea of seeing a statue of myself, but the wrinkle vanished when I saw Chris place the first correct piece.

Crap.

Crap, crap, crap.

If Rhett didn't win, I was fucked. And not in a good way. I had feelings for the bastard. Deep feelings. Feelings I wasn't anywhere near ready to acknowledge, but feelings that were definitely still there.

I slid to the edge of my bench, praying to whatever the hell was in the sky—if anything *was* up there—to help Rhett win. I wasn't much for relying on other people or things, but I literally had no other choice.

"This game is so screwed up," I told Jordan, my heart hammering in my chest.

"Wouldn't be quite as bad if you didn't go getting attached to one of the contestants."

I smacked him on the arm, and he chuckled, not bothering to pretend it hurt.

Chris got two more pieces.

I started to sweat.

It was cloudy and windy outside, but not raining.

For once, I wanted the rain. Anything to erase the wetness gathering in my pits and on my back.

I was so close to getting everything I wanted.

And so, so close to losing it.

The puzzle went on, slowly.

Chris was halfway through, and I was fervently whispering *please* to anyone or anything that might be listening, when Rhett finally got his first piece.

A bolt of gratitude raced down my spine.

It vanished as quickly as it had hit.

But Rhett was moving, then.

The pieces went down quickly as he worked through the sections he'd made.

Kyle got a few, though his sorted piles didn't look terribly organized.

Travis had about a dozen up, but they didn't look correct next to the other guys'.

Rhett finally caught Chris halfway up my puzzle's face.

"I'm going to rip my fucking hair out," I told Jordan, breathing rapidly.

"Same."

I would've grabbed his hand if I thought he would let me, but given the game, that was an instant no.

Chris put another piece in.

Rhett did too.

Chris got another.

Rhett got two more.

My stomach clenched so painfully, there was a real chance I was going to throw up.

Suddenly, Chris put three pieces in.

Fuck.

Fuck, fuck, fuck.

He only had one left. One piece. On the table beside him.

Rhett still had four.

He was so laser-focused on the puzzle, he didn't know how close Chris was.

My heart started to sink.

I never cried, but my damn eyes flooded with tears.

That was it.

I was going to have to mate with Kyle.

Travis whooped loudly as Chris picked up the final piece, glancing over at Rhett's puzzle.

Then, he looked at me.

Rhett put another piece in, and another.

After a long moment, Chris looked back at his puzzle and feigned trying to place it. From the angle I was sitting, I could clearly see that he had it backward. "Shit! It doesn't fit!" He dropped his last piece and pulled three out.

My stomach clenched tighter.

My eyes blurred with water.

He hadn't messed the puzzle up.

He'd been a heartbeat away from winning.

Travis snarled and swore, but the words didn't even register in my mind.

Because Rhett put the final puzzle pieces in, and Jordan stood.

My mind was in a daze as he announced the winner.

As I got to my feet and ran the three steps to Rhett.

As he caught me and hauled me off the sand, holding me so tightly I stopped breathing for a moment.

He held me steadily against his chest as he lowered me back to my feet, my heart still pounding.

While Jordan announced the reward, I looked at Chris.

His lips curved upward when he met my gaze.

I mouthed a soft thank you, and he winked.

Rhett whisked me off to the speedboat nearby moments later, and my heartbeat finally slowed as he held me close through the ride.

We made it.

We made it.

We made it.

RHETT

I'D WON the challenge by a matter of seconds.

Seconds.

Fuck, I might never sleep again.

Or let go of the woman I was all but clinging to.

The speedboat carried us toward the same yacht Molly and Cameron had stayed in after that particular challenge in their season. I had Erin basically glued to my front while the boat crashed through the growing waves that accompanied the brewing storm.

A yacht didn't seem like a great place to be during a tropical storm, but the Society would move us if it grew too dangerous.

Hopefully.

I let out a shaky breath and buried my nose in Erin's hair, closing my eyes.

That had been close.

Too close.

I hoped to never see another fucking puzzle in my life.

seventeen

ERIN

THE YACHT ROCKED FAR MORE than I was comfortable with as we boarded. The storm around us was getting worse, not better, which I didn't think bode well for our reward.

Sure enough, those working on the boat looked nervous as they ushered us toward a table that was set up in a small room connected to the kitchen.

"I hope they're driving this thing toward land," I muttered to Rhett, as I sat down in the chair he pulled out for me.

He pulled our server to the side. "Is there an alternate plan if the storm doesn't blow over quickly?"

It wasn't going to blow over.

We'd been living on an island, through terrible storms, long enough that I was sure of that.

The man nodded. "We're headed toward a dock now. There's a hotel near it that you'll be moved to."

Rhett nodded and took the seat across from mine.

I grabbed the table to stay in my seat when there was a particularly rough wave.

Rhett's eyes flashed, and he was on his feet again in a heartbeat. He lifted me off the chair, then set me on his lap when he sat back down.

"I'm fine," I protested.

"I'm not." His nose brushed my neck.

I leaned back against him, and his grip tightened as another massive wave rocked us.

"That was too close," he said quietly.

"At least it's over." I closed my eyes.

He kissed my throat lightly.

It occurred to me that he hadn't been looking at his competition at all, and I bit my lip. I didn't want to hurt him with the truth, but he deserved to know just in case it came up again.

Even if it didn't, our season would be on TV eventually. It wasn't going to be a secret.

"You know Chris let you win, right?" I asked.

Rhett didn't reply immediately.

I'd take that as a no.

"He was down to the last piece. Travis was cheering. He acted like he'd placed them wrong, and pulled a few out to give you time to win."

"Damn." Rhett's voice was low, but I couldn't label whatever emotion was in it. We hadn't spent enough time together for that. "I owe him."

"*We* owe him."

His grip on my waist tightened. "Are we a team now, Chaos?"

"I think so."

The server brought out two massive plates of food just as the boat rocked hard.

I reached toward the man, but it was no use.

He lost his footing, and went down hard.

The plates shattered and the food went everywhere, but I was more worried about the guy, who didn't get up right away.

Two other workers hurried to help him before I could stand up, so we stayed in our seat. All three of them apologized to us as they hurried out, and Rhett called behind them,

"We'll eat at the hotel. Everyone needs to sit down and stay safe."

His lips brushed my throat again as the boat rocked fiercely.

For once, I was glad my stomach was empty. If there'd been any food in me, I would've been fighting serious nausea.

As it was, my body wasn't thrilled with the boat's intense motion.

"I hope it's not a long way to the dock," I said, turning my head so I could tuck my face against Rhett's neck. He adjusted my position on his lap, giving me better access.

I wrapped my arms around him as I pressed my forehead to his skin, closing my eyes.

Something in my chest settled.

Rhett *was* the right choice. There was a lot we didn't know about each other and hadn't been able to discuss, but I was sure of that. And that was what mattered.

IT FELT like hours had passed by the time the boat was finally docked. The storm was still raging, so Rhett flew me off the boat before he and Jordan carried a bunch of others to solid land too.

When the boat was empty of everyone who didn't want to stay on, Rhett tucked me against his side as we followed Jordan to the hotel. Luckily, they were expecting us, and had a private table ready for us at the back of the restaurant.

Both of us ignored the stares and whispers that echoed as we walked through the restaurant.

Rhett's arm remained steady around my waist.

When we sat down, we slipped into one side of the booth together so we could remain out of sight. Our waitress didn't bat an eye at our state of dress or the fact that we were soaked, and took our orders.

When she walked away, I leaned my head against Rhett's shoulder. "I wish we could fast-forward through the next few days," I admitted. "Especially if it's just going to keep raining. I don't know if I'll survive."

"We'll make it." Rhett's voice left no room for question.

The restaurant was so noisy that neither of us said much while we ate. We worked through the food quickly, heading to our room as soon as we were done.

RHETT CLOSED the door behind us, leaving Jordan on the other side.

My gaze moved over the room. It was small but nice, with pretty wood paneling on one of the walls while the others were a comfortable shade of cream. There was a fae-sized bed, a human-sized bathroom, and not much else.

"Too bad we didn't bring our robes," I remarked, slipping my raincoat off my shoulders. My clothes had never truly dried since I got it, so they were drenched beneath it.

I still loved it, though.

Rhett took the coat from me and hung it in the small closet.

I murmured a *thank you*, and he pressed a kiss to my shoulder.

My eyes closed with the soft touch, and he stepped up behind me, wrapping his arms around me.

I didn't have words for the soft intensity of feeling him against me that way.

Bliss?

Peace?

Joy?

Whatever it was, it made my throat swell and my eyes sting a little.

Maybe I just felt safe.

Or loved.

He didn't love me, of course. We hadn't known each other for long enough.

But that didn't mean I couldn't *feel* loved, did it?

It was a foreign feeling for me, so I wasn't really sure. I'd never had anyone care about me like that. My mom had loved me in her own way, but she'd cared more about her boyfriend. I'd never been a priority for her, or anyone else.

So what would it feel like to be Rhett's?

"Will you shower with me?" he murmured, his voice low and soft.

There was vulnerability in it.

My throat swelled more.

What if I hurt him?

I didn't know how to love any more than I knew how to *be* loved. What if I ended up just as bad as his ex?

Despite my fear, I nodded.

He walked us into the bathroom, his arms still around my body as we moved. There was a large shower/tub combo to my left, with one of those fabric shower curtains I'd always hated, but I didn't give a damn.

I'd never showered with anyone. Not even for sex.

Granted, my sex life had been short-lived. I'd barely been nineteen when my blood was tested, and the *world-nearly-ending* thing put a damper on sex for pretty much everyone my age.

Rhett turned the shower on, and I looked up as water started flowing from the ceiling.

Our time in the spa had proven that I loved a good, fancy showerhead.

Rhett's fingers skimmed my bare ribcage lightly before hooking in the bottom hem of my sports bra. He was giving me time to turn him down, or back out.

Time I didn't need.

I lifted my arms, and he peeled the fabric over my skin. His chest rumbled when my breasts fell free, and he dropped my bra so he could take them in his hands.

Closing my eyes, I leaned back against his chest while he played with my nipples. My body warmed, wetness gathering between my thighs as he teased the sensitive buds.

"You're beautiful." His words were rough in my ear, and goosebumps broke out on my arms.

There was no one to interrupt us this time.

No one to stop us.

No one else I might be forced to mate with.

Just me, and Rhett.

He released my breasts, sliding his hands down the curve of my waist until he found the top of my shorts.

My entire body clenched as he slid them down my thighs.

The fabric made an obnoxious sound as it hit the floor, but neither of us commented on it. Neither of us *cared*.

I eased away from him, turning so we faced each other. The top of my head didn't even hit the bottom of his chin, but he tilted his head, and I leaned mine too. Our eyes were locked as I pushed his shorts down. His cock sprang free, and I finally looked away just so I could stare at him.

Damn, he was huge.

My body flushed hotter.

I wrapped my fingers around his erection and dragged them over the length lightly, earning a low rumble.

"Have you ever showered with anyone before?" he asked.

Something in his voice told me he was going to think violent thoughts if I said yes.

And that made me think violent thoughts about the woman *he'd* probably showered with.

"No," I admitted, stroking him again just so I could hear his chest rumble more. "Have you?"

"Only once."

"And?"

"And what?"

"And how did it go?" My possessiveness was showing. I knew that. I just couldn't help it.

I wanted to have our firsts together. I didn't want to know he'd enjoyed himself with another woman before—or consider that she might be better than me.

I'd just have to upstage her.

Considering she'd never touched his wings, I *could* do that. And knowing I could made me feel slightly better.

"She let me get her off but didn't touch me," Rhett admitted.

"Bitch."

He chuckled. "I don't expect any more from you than I did from her, Chaos. I don't touch you because I want—"

I cut him off. "*Start* expecting more from me than you did from her. I'm not her. Accept it."

I stroked him again, a little rougher, and earned a growl for it.

He grabbed me by the waist, lifting me into the shower as he stepped beneath the water. It was blazing hot as it fell over us, and he swore again as he stepped closer, reaching behind me to turn the temperature down as he blocked me from the burn of it.

I stroked him again, and he growled into my hair, gripping my hand over his erection. "Slow down, Chaos."

I'd never seen him lose control, but I wanted to.

Badly.

"Why should I slow down?"

"You don't have to touch me like this just because Kellie didn't," he gritted out. "That's not—"

"That's *not* why I'm touching you."

His gaze was hot, but I could see in his eyes that he didn't believe me.

With my free hand, I took one of his wrists and slipped it between my thighs. His fingers brushed my wetness, and my body clenched again.

"I'm touching you because it turns me on," I said. "Yeah, my possessive side is glad she didn't touch you, and I'd kind of like to mark you as mine by doing it. But I *want to*, Rhett. I want to watch you come undone. I want to see your release on my skin, I want to make you wild with need, I want to—"

The breath rushed out of me as my back met the shower's wall.

Rhett's chest rose and fell quickly, his cock throbbing hard in my hand as our gazes remained locked.

Thrill raced up my spine.

In the spa, I'd been set on getting that out of him. The dominance. The determination. The certainty.

He'd been holding himself back, resisting the urges I desperately wanted him to give in to.

If we were going to be together, I wanted us to be together freely. Passionately. Without holding back.

"Tell me how you want me to touch you," I said, without looking away.

He let out an unsteady breath, and finally released his grip on my hand. I didn't stroke him again, though. I waited.

One of his hands was still between my thighs, but it wasn't moving.

He planted the other on the wall of the shower, just to the side of my head.

"Put a hand on my wing," he finally gritted out, his shoulders rolling as his wings unfurled. The water fell against them, and his cock jerked slightly.

My thighs clenched, and his fingers lifted closer to my core.

I pressed my free hand to his wing, the other on his cock, and waited.

He throbbed again.

His eyes closed, his jaw clenching. "Slowly. Touch me slowly."

"I'm going to need more instructions than that, Rhetti." My voice was soft.

Hot.

A little playful, too. The nickname emphasized that.

His cock jerked in my grasp. "Drag your fingers lightly over my wing, close to where it meets my back. It's not as sensitive there. Work my cock slowly."

I followed his orders.

One hand stroked his cock lightly. The other teased his wing.

My hand grew slick with the start of his pleasure.

"Fuck me," he swore, his whole body tight as he fought off his release.

"Is that a command?"

I jerked him a little harder, and he grabbed my hand again.

His eyes flew open, hot and intense. "*Soft*, Chaos."

My lips curved wickedly. "Is that a threat?"

There was a shift in his eyes that told me he was about to shut himself down.

I repeated the motion with his hand over mine, and he swore loudly, gripping me tighter.

"I *want* it to be a threat, Rhetti. Stop holding yourself back. We both know you would never hurt me."

His chest rose and fell rapidly.

Our gazes remained locked.

And slowly, I tried to repeat the motion.

His grip tightened on my hand, holding me in place. We were squeezing the hell out of his cock, but he throbbed so hard, it clearly didn't hurt.

"I said soft, Chaos. Touch me like that again and I'll have to pin your hand above your head. I'm not ready to come yet."

That was a start.

He swore, his fingers curling between my thighs. "That turns you on?"

"I like you dominant."

He released my hand over his cock and placed it back on the wall beside my head. The shower's water was still falling behind Rhett, but we were both too used to rain to notice.

"But I also like to push you," I said, flashing him a grin and working his cock hard and fast.

He snarled another curse, his hips jerking as he thrusted into my fist, losing control entirely. His release coated my hand and abdomen, his fingers pressing against my clit lightly enough to make me crazy but too light to get me off.

The moment wasn't about me, so I didn't care.

I was too busy watching the intensity of the gorgeous man's pleasure.

His chest heaved, his eyes burning as his cock jerked with the last of his release. "Chaos," He rumbled, the word low and hot and angry.

"You knew who I was before you ever propositioned me, Rhetti." I squeezed him lightly. "When you've recovered, we'll—"

He grabbed one of my thighs, opening me up as he stepped closer.

The motion forced me to release his cock.

When I looked down, I found him just as hard as he'd been a moment later.

Did he not need to recover?

I'd never seen him get off, so—

He shifted, losing the wings and horns.

At the same time, he lined the tip of his cock up with my entrance, and thrust.

My breathing stopped as he filled me.

And filled me.

And filled me.

"Shit," I choked out.

"You want me dominant?" His growl vibrated my chest. "You'll get me dominant."

His hand caught my hips, and he dragged a thumb over my clit, making me gasp.

As I did, his mouth crashed into mine.

He didn't kiss me softly.

He didn't taste me, or tease me.

He devoured me, taking what he wanted exactly the way I'd told him to. His tongue was hot and demanding, and his free hand grabbed my ass, lifting me higher.

The change in angle had me gasping again.

He kissed me through it, using the new height difference to his advantage as he pulled me down over him, then lifted me again.

The motion was rough.

Hard.

Perfect.

I unraveled with a cry into his mouth, but he didn't stop fucking me. He worked my clit with his thumb until I came again, my body tightening around him.

He roared with me, filling me with his release until it was dripping down my thighs.

He was everything.

eighteen

ERIN

RHETT HELD me against the wall as we both caught our breath. When he set me back down on my feet, his hands found my hips and he turned me around so my back was to his chest again.

Then, he grabbed the little trial bottle of shampoo. "I want to wash your hair."

"Mmkay." I was too worn out to care.

After the adrenaline of the challenge and the storm, followed by the pure relaxation of my orgasms, he could do whatever he wanted to me.

And letting him wash my hair would save me the effort, so it was a win-win situation.

My eyes closed as he tugged my hairband free and buried his fingers in the tangled strands. He wasn't in any hurry, slowly massaging my scalp as he worked the shampoo in.

I was going to be a calm, happy puddle by the time he was done.

When he rinsed the shampoo out and repeated the process with conditioner, my back and ass were pressed against his front. He had hardened again at some point in the process, but neither of us acknowledged it. If there was going to be more sex, it wasn't going to be happening until after the shower.

We'd been stuck on an island far too long to not have that level of self-restraint.

After he washed the conditioner out, he slowly scrubbed the rest of my body with shower gel.

It was blissful in a way nothing else I'd ever experienced could compare.

To lean against someone like that, to trust them with my body that way... it was unreal.

"Is it supposed to be this intense between us?" I asked, my voice soft.

"What do you mean?" His was quiet too, but more laid-back than mine.

"I don't know."

He ran his hands over my abdomen, slowly washing my belly. "It wasn't like this with Kellie, if that's what you mean," he said. "I never felt like I could trust her. I never felt like we were *friends*. We were together, but there was no intimacy. Not emotionally."

I nodded. "I've never been in a relationship, but yeah. I feel like that too. I've never really... trusted anyone before. But I trust you. I think. Mostly."

He kissed my neck, and I tilted my head to the side to give him better access. "Considering we've been on an island for weeks, playing a game that prevented us from doing and saying what we wanted, I'd be concerned if you trusted me implicitly right now."

My lips curved upward. "You think I'll get there, though?"

I really didn't want to hurt him. And I didn't want to end up in a marriage where my husband resented me for being myself. I would never trust as easily as some people could. I would never be entirely free from my past.

"I do, but there's no rush. I'll be here whether you expect me to be or not." He kissed my neck again. "I want you, Chaos. I need you. I'm not leaving you, no matter what."

My eyes stung with tears.

He may as well have proclaimed his love, because to me?

That was love.

He accepted my limits, he didn't expect me to change, and he wasn't walking away.

What more could anyone need?

"Thank you," I whispered, dashing at my eye with the side of my hand. I didn't *feel* any tears falling, but I wasn't risking it. I did *not* cry.

"Don't thank me for caring." He ran his slick hands over my hips. "Kiss me instead."

I turned around in his arms and grabbed his face, rising onto my tiptoes to kiss him.

He kissed me back until I pulled away and turned around again, biting my swollen bottom lip lightly to hide my smile.

I was happy.

Stupidly, ridiculously happy.

When we were done washing up, we dried off and made our way to the bed. There were no spare clothes, so we climbed in naked.

I was exhausted enough from the events and emotions of the day that I just sprawled across Rhett, not bothering with the TV. One of his arms draped over my waist, and the other hand found my ass.

For the first time in ages, I didn't need an illusion to fall asleep feeling safe and content.

LOUD POUNDING on the door woke us.

I jerked upward, peeling my body off Rhett's.

His grip on my ass tightened, his eyes bleary as he looked around the room.

Jordan knocked again before pushing it open. "The tropical storm looks like it's on its way to becoming a hurricane near the *Survival* island. We've got a group of air and water fae heading out to try to prevent it, but the last few days of the game are getting cut. We're meeting the remaining contestants on a stretch of beach near here. It's time to choose a mate, Erin."

My stomach clenched.

As much as I wanted the game to end, and knew who I was going to choose, making the choice was still a big deal.

And sealing the bond?

That was more than a little terrifying.

I wasn't even sure how it would happen, or what I would have to do.

What if there was blood involved?

Or—

"It's going to be fine," Rhett said, meeting my gaze. "Close the door, Jordan. We need to get dressed."

Jordan shut it, and I let out a shaky breath.

Rhett took my face between his hands and tilted my head toward his until our foreheads met.

"I won't let anything happen to you," he said, his voice quiet but steady.

"I know." Somehow, it was true.

"What are you afraid of?"

"A mate bond," I admitted. "Getting wings. Blood sacrifices, or some shit like that."

"*Blood sacrifices?*"

"How else would I become fae?"

"With magic." He brushed a few strands of slightly damp hair off my face. "We'll have sex and say vows to each other. My magic will become yours, and change you in the process."

"Oh."

Rhett's eyes softened with one of his small, quick smiles. "No blood or sacrificing. Just sex."

"I can probably handle that," I said.

He brushed his lips against mine for a quick kiss. I leaned in, deepening it, and he rumbled against me before pulling away. "We'll pick this back up after the game is over, alright?"

"Okay." I nodded, some of my fear fading away.

He kissed me again, then stood, lifting me off the bed with him. I crashed into his chest, and he squeezed my hip lightly, steadying me as he set me back down on my feet at the edge of the bed.

I looked at the bathroom floor for my clothes as he walked in, but didn't see them.

They weren't where I'd left them.

Hmm.

I was momentarily distracted by the sight of his perfect ass as he stepped into his shorts.

Rhett came out a moment later with my clothes in his hand. "I hung them up to dry after you fell asleep."

"You stayed awake?" My eyebrows lifted, but I accepted the clothes.

"Not for long."

I pulled the familiar fabric on. It was still slightly damp, but much drier than it would've been if it had remained on the floor.

"Thank you." I went up on my tiptoes to kiss him again, but Jordan knocked before I could.

Rhett leaned down and brushed his lips against mine anyway. "Just a little longer, and all of this will be over."

"Finally."

"Finally," he agreed.

With that, we made our way out through the door.

THE WIND WHIPPED my hair around as Rhett flew me to the beach. Jordan was right behind us, staying close the whole time. Rain fell lightly, and the wind made it blur my vision.

We reached the other guys soon enough, and found them sitting on the sand, drenched and exhausted. Travis was gone, so he'd been the final man voted off the island.

Kyle and Chris stood up, and Rhett released me after a final squeeze to my hip. He stepped into place beside them.

I made my way to Jordan's side, stopping in front of them.

My gaze moved over the three men.

Honestly?

I liked all of them for the most part. I trusted that none of them would hurt me if I chose them. I wouldn't have been *afraid* to mate with any of them.

But I *wanted* Rhett.

So, the choice was a simple one.

"Thanks to the weather, the game has officially been cut short," Jordan said, looking at the men. "Any final words?"

"No." Chris shook his head. "I don't think there's anything to say."

"Nah." Kyle winked at me. "Erin obviously made her mind up already."

I bit my lip to hold back a smile.

As obnoxious as he was, he was a good guy.

All of us looked at Rhett.

"Anything to say?" Jordan asked him.

Rhett's focus was entirely on my face, his lips curved in a small smile that was just for me. "She knows."

I couldn't hide my smile.

"Well, Erin?" Jordan turned back to me, but I was already crossing the sand, back to the man I wanted.

"I choose Rhett," I called over my shoulder.

He caught me before I reached him, pulling me into his arms and kissing me.

Jordan must've said something else, but I didn't hear him.

I was too lost in Rhett.

nineteen

ERIN

WE WERE SUPPOSED to be taken straight to a mansion on a deserted island, where we could spend two weeks alone together, sealing the bond.

The storm made that an impossibility. Jordan let us know that the Society offered to rent us a vacation home in a city nearby, or that we could choose to go to Rhett's house early.

We'd both been done with tropical islands, and gone with the latter option.

So, Rhett and I boarded the private plane that had carried us to the island.

Jordan and the other guys went to wherever they were going to prepare for the next season. It would be starting in a few days, so the guys would all just spend the time feasting and sleeping in a hotel.

Realizing that the game was over felt surreal.

Accepting that Rhett was going to be my mate?

That would take time.

Possibly a *lot* of time.

I looked around the interior of the plane. Though it was elegant, there was nothing inside but large armchairs. No couches. Nothing resembling a bed.

The chairs *did* recline.

But the way Rhett's arm had remained wrapped around my waist since I chose him made me think he wasn't going to let go of me with any amount of enthusiasm.

"Where do you want to sit?" I asked.

He answered by lifting me off my feet, sitting down in the largest chair, and setting me on his lap.

The way his body nearly engulfed mine made me feel small and feminine.

Warm, too.

And maybe a little bit loved.

His lips met my throat, and I closed my eyes as he kissed me lightly. "It's going to be a long flight."

"I know," I whispered.

"You should sleep through most of it."

"So should you."

Rhett made a noise of agreement. "When we're home, we'll figure everything else out. No overthinking."

"No overthinking," I agreed, though my stomach was a little tight.

We took off a few minutes later, and sure enough, I fell asleep almost as soon as we were in the sky.

AFTER A MONTH ON AN ISLAND, I had no problem at all sleeping in the arms of a gorgeous fae man while there was working air conditioning.

I didn't wake up until the plane landed, and when I did, Rhett's arms were firm enough around me that I didn't budge despite the jostling.

"We made it?" I asked, my voice heavy with sleep.

"Yep." Rhett kissed the top of my head. "Time to head home."

Home.

It was a strange concept to me. I wasn't sure I'd ever truly felt at home, anywhere.

Certainly not during my childhood. There had been some measure of peace after my mom and her boyfriend died, but the world was a shitshow at that point.

I'd been trying to figure out a way to escape being compatible mates with a fae since the world finally calmed down, so I hadn't let myself get settled then.

But I felt more comfortable in Rhett's arms than I could ever remember feeling before.

Maybe I belonged with him. Maybe he was supposed to be my home.

Damn, that sounded cheesy.

But I couldn't stop myself from thinking it might be true.

We walked off the plane a few minutes later, and were in the back seat of an armored vehicle a few minutes after that.

"Do we really need this much protection?" I murmured to Rhett, as we pulled away from the small airport after buckling up. Rhett was sitting in the middle of the bench, as if it wasn't the least-comfortable spot in the vehicle, and I was on his right.

His hand landed on my thigh, his grip light though the touch was clearly possessive. "No. It's just the Society's protocols when it comes to the shows. It's better to be too protective than to risk anyone's life."

"Is that why you made me buckle my seatbelt before you left my old apartment?"

His lips curved upward. "No. I made you buckle because you looked like you were going to bail the moment I turned away, and the seatbelt's click would give me more time to react."

I snorted. "Clever asshole."

He chuckled. "I'm not a beginner."

I leaned my head against his shoulder, watching the scenery around us as we drove. The coastal town was gorgeous, both quaint and cozy.

I'd never lived outside a big city, so that was going to be new. I couldn't say I'd miss the noise and hustle. Especially after living nearly a month on the *Survival* island.

"Let's never go out in the rain again," I said, my gaze lingering on the way the sun's rays kissed the buildings around us.

"Agreed."

We stayed quiet for the last fifteen minutes of the drive.

Soon enough, the vehicle was parked in front of a nice beach home that I recognized from the pictures Christina had sent.

Rhett's house was beautiful.

Large windows made the ocean view such a permanent fixture that I barely noticed anything else.

"So you own this place?" I asked, standing on the sidewalk in front of it. "We haven't talked about finances. Or much else in the real-world."

We probably should've done that.

Shit.

I didn't know what our life would look like together, or what he expected from me after we were mated. Or—

He stepped up behind me, his body steady against my back. I let out a quick breath at the sudden pressure.

His hand landed on my hip, and I couldn't stop myself from leaning against him a little. "We'll talk about everything," he said.

The words were simple, but eased my fear.

"I don't know how to have a relationship," I admitted.

"I don't know how to have a *successful* relationship. We'll figure it out together."

That did sound good.

He led me up the steps to the front door, his chest still against my back as we moved together. When he typed in a code to unlock the large double doors, he didn't try to hide it from me.

1201.

"My mom's birthday," he explained. "We always had the same codes for everything. We gave each other privacy, but having the same code would make an emergency much easier."

My heart squeezed at the simple intimacy of that.

Sharing codes.

I'd never even had a key to my mom's place. When I got home on the odd days she bothered locking the door, I had to sit on the doorstep until she got home. I'd waited for hours, sometimes.

It had been dangerous, and made me feel like I didn't matter to her. It was a damn miracle nothing bad had ever happened to me when I was outside.

Then again, the inside of that apartment hadn't been any safer.

"You guys were close," I said, as we stepped inside the house.

My eyes moved over the interior.

It wasn't a mansion, but everything was oversized. The halls and doorways were insanely wide, and nothing was placed too close together. The few decorations looked big and heavy.

"It's beautiful," I said.

"It's yours." Rhett lowered his lips to my shoulder and kissed it. No one had given me a shirt, and I'd left my favorite raincoat in the hotel, so all I had on was a sports bra.

"We're not technically mates yet."

"That will be remedied soon."

My lower belly tightened at the certainty in his voice.

And the promise of what it meant.

Sex.

Hot sex.

Permanently hot sex.

Changing.

Becoming a fae.

Growing wings.

"Is everything in here so open because of your wings?" I asked, changing the subject abruptly.

"Yes. It feels more natural to remain in fae form sometimes."

I nodded, biting my lip. "What's it like to have wings?"

"About the same as not having wings. They become a part of you."

I nodded again. "Can you show me where my room is?"

"*Our* room?"

"Right."

He led me through the house, pointing out an office, two spare rooms, the kitchen, and finally, *our* bedroom.

It was massive, with a monstrously large bed that would fit two fae in their winged forms. The furniture looked sturdy and comfortable. The art on the walls featured more beaches.

"You love the beach, huh?"

"I do," Rhett admitted. "Though I'd prefer never to set foot on the *Survival* island again."

I bit my lip to stop myself from smiling.

We definitely agreed on that.

"I'm going to shower," I said. "I still feel covered in sand. Can I borrow some clean clothes?"

"Of course. The Society should have your things here in the next day or two."

I nodded, nerves and uncertainty still running rampant in my chest. I fought like hell not to let Rhett see it.

He stepped into the closet while I turned the water on in the monstrous shower, letting it warm up while I looked at myself in the mirror.

I hadn't paid attention the night before, when we were in the hotel, so my appearance caught me off guard.

I was thinner.

Slightly more tan, but mostly a little redder, since that's what my body liked to do under the sun. I'd used tons of sunscreen, and stayed in the shade as much as possible, but I'd still been living on an island.

Though the weight loss made my face thinner, the experience had made my eyes sort of... softer.

More vulnerable.

The small woman in the mirror was *not* the strong, hard creature I'd been the day Rhett drove me to the airport.

I'd changed, even without any magic to turn me into a fae. I'd been forced to.

Rhett stepped up behind me and set a neatly folded pile of

clothes on the bathroom's countertop. His hand caught my hip again, and my gaze followed it down in the mirror.

And lingered.

Something welled up in my chest. I didn't know what to label it, and I wasn't entirely comfortable with the feeling. It was too new.

"What are you thinking?" Rhett asked, his voice quiet.

I met his gaze in the mirror. "My tits are tiny."

He chuckled, his free hand finding one of my breasts and squeezing lightly. "They're perfect."

"As soon as I start eating, they're going to fill out again."

"Then I should get to feeding you, immediately. What kind of cake is your favorite?"

I snorted. "You want to fatten me up so my boobs grow?"

"I want to get you healthy again after watching you starve for nearly a month," he corrected. "But if your breasts grow in the process, you won't hear any complaints from me."

"Shocking," I drawled.

He squeezed my tit again. "Let me shower with you."

My mind went back to our shower in the hotel, and my face warmed. I watched the red spread over my cheeks in the mirror. "I need a few minutes to think. Next time?"

He dipped his head. "What do you need to think about."

"Everything."

His forehead creased.

I stepped out of his arms and grabbed his elbow, leading him to the bathroom's large sliding doors. They were similar to the barn doors that had been trendy long ago, but were a more modern version.

"I'll come find you when I'm done." Leaving him outside the door, I closed it.

Or closed it as much as was possible, given that it didn't have a lock or anything. Really, it was more like a privacy divider than a door.

Standing just on the other side of it, I closed my eyes and let out a slow breath.

I'd never really managed to think my way through something. My brain didn't work like that. If it did, I hadn't figured out how. I usually just had to ignore my feelings until they went away. If I could avoid them long enough, I could seal the bond with Rhett and be forced to figure everything else out as it came up.

That was probably ideal.

I heard footsteps on the other side of the door, and tilted my head closer so I could hear Rhett walk away.

But, as soon as the footsteps moved away, they returned.

My forehead creased as I listened.

Close, then far.

Close, then far.

Close, then far.

Ohhh.

He was pacing.

He wasn't as skilled at ignoring my emotions as I was. And didn't realize why I needed space.

I didn't want to tell him, though.

When he really learned how to embrace his dominant side, he would just step back into the bathroom and demand to talk to me. Maybe we'd even learn how to work through things that way.

But at the moment, he didn't seem ready to push me.

And I wasn't going to offer to help with that when it came to feelings I didn't really understand myself.

I wasn't the kind of girl who would ever survive being married or mated to a timid guy. If Rhett and I were going to make things work, he had to be honest with both me and himself, and speak up when he wanted to speak up.

He wasn't there yet, but I was pretty damn sure he'd get there.

So, I finally stepped into the shower. After the water washed most of my sand away, I sniffed all the different products, enjoying the yummy, masculine scents. I'd never smelled any of them on Rhett, considering where we'd been living, but I kind of looked forward to it.

I scrubbed my scalp with shampoo viciously, then loaded conditioner onto the strands before rubbing my entire body down with shower gel.

I was almost finished rinsing the conditioner out when the sliding door finally moved.

Surprise lifted my eyebrows as Rhett stepped inside, his gaze intense. Instead of speaking, he stepped out of his shorts and boxers, then joined me in the shower.

I stepped back to give him space.

He didn't like that, and reached for my hips.

I took another step back, holding out my hands. "You're sandy. I finally got clean."

"I'll wash you again." He captured my hips and tugged me closer, until my bare chest was pressed against his.

"I told you, I need time to think."

"Think out loud, then." His grip on my hips was possessive.

Determined, too.

He wasn't letting me go until he was satisfied with my response. And as much as I didn't want to talk to him, I respected that.

Grudgingly.

"Or we could just..." I trailed off, going up on my tiptoes so I could kiss him.

He kissed me back, walking me two steps backward until he had me pinned to the wall.

Then, he ended the kiss. "I want to know what you're thinking, Chaos."

I sighed, leaning back against the tile wall and shutting my eyes.

He waited.

"I'm thinking that a lot of things are going to change, and that's terrifying," I said, my voice quiet. "I'm thinking that I have no idea what our life together is going to look like. I'm thinking that we should date for another year or two before we seal the bond, but you're not going to be okay with it. I'm thinking that this marriage shit is really big, and really permanent."

He didn't answer right away.

I squeezed my eyes shut a little tighter.

"I'd give you more time if I could, Chaos," Rhett finally said, his voice quiet but genuine. "I just don't have time to give."

My stomach clenched.

My entire body clenched.

He was dying. I'd forgotten he was dying.

"Things are going to change for both of us," he said. "But we're going to change together. Yes, it'll be harder for you, since you're growing wings, but we'll adapt together. Grow together. Figure shit out together."

I let out a shaky breath. "I barely recognize myself after all the rain and starvation. I'm weaker, now. I looked *vulnerable*."

"Being vulnerable takes a hell of a lot more courage than any amount of coldness," Rhett said bluntly. "It's easy to push people away. It's hard to let them in. Physically, you're weaker now, but mentally? Emotionally? You survived, and you came out stronger for it."

"I don't know if that's true."

Rhett captured my face in his hands and tilted it back until our eyes met. "*I* know it's true. Trust me."

I did.

I trusted him.

As insane as that was.

I finally dipped my head in a small nod, and he kissed me.

His mouth was soft, but the kiss wasn't slow or gentle.

It was rough.

Fierce.

Delicious.

I hooked a leg around his hip, and Rhett's chest rumbled against mine. One of his hands found my ass, lifting me higher and changing the angle a bit.

I sucked in a breath against his mouth as the thick length of his erection pressed against my clit.

Moving my hips just a little, I lined his tip up with my entrance as we kissed.

He growled into my mouth, grabbing my other thigh and wrapping it around his waist as he lifted me higher.

I gasped against his lips as he pulled me down over his cock, filling me fast and hard.

The shower spun around me as I breathed hard, trying desperately to adjust to the feel of him inside me. I hadn't eaten anything, which didn't make me any less faint.

But I was used to starvation.

I'd ignore the shit out of it if it meant having Rhett inside me like he was.

He hauled me out of the shower without bothering to turn the water off or pull out of me. I didn't even hear the door close behind us.

My hair dripped down my back and ass before he set me down on my back on the bed. Then, it soaked the blankets.

Rhett's eyes burned over my bare figure as he leaned over me, his hands on either side of my head.

"Shift," I said. "I want to touch your wings."

His cock throbbed inside me. "If I shift, we're sealing the bond." He rocked his hips slowly, smoothly, dragging a ragged gasp out of me. "There's time for that later. Right now, I'm taking you like this."

My heels dug into the thick muscles on his ass as my hips arched to meet his next, slow thrust. "Mmkay."

The word was strained.

I didn't have the mental willpower to argue.

He worked himself in and out of me slowly, every inch of his thick cock hitting that perfect spot inside me as he moved.

It was insane.

Intense.

Incredible.

I unraveled with a moan.

Panting, sweating, and rocking, I came down from the high while he continued to move inside me.

The sensation was unlike anything I'd ever experienced before.

As amazing as it was, it was intimate in a way I didn't have words to describe.

It didn't feel like he was fucking me; it felt like he was making love to me.

I met Rhett's gaze, and found something I hadn't seen in it before.

Something like *devotion.*

Maybe even something like love.

"You're unreal," I breathed, my hips still moving with his.

"You're unbelievable." He unwrapped one of my legs from around his waist and lifted it up to his shoulder.

My lips parted at the change in sensation.

He repeated the motion with my second leg, then lifted my hips slightly as he started thrusting in a little harder, and a little faster.

A cry tore through me at the sudden climax that hit, and I felt every inch of him as my body tightened around him, squeezing.

He swore, his cock throbbing violently as he lost control inside me.

We were both panting as the pleasure faded, but he was still hard as a rock.

He wanted more.

I did too.

"Will I ever get enough of you?" I moaned, as he moved just a little.

"I hope not." He lowered my thighs from his shoulders. "I want you on your hands and knees."

Lust made my lower body clench. "I've never been fucked that way."

"I've never fucked anyone that way."

"It's another first for both of us, then." I moved my hips, sliding him out of me before I rolled over to my hands and knees. The world spun again a little—I really needed to eat —but food was far from a priority.

Rhett rumbled when I lifted my ass in the air, and he gripped it in both hands. When he parted my cheeks, I sucked in a breath.

He dragged his thumb over my back entrance, using the slickness of our combined release to make the motion smooth.

My hips jerked at the touch.

"I'm going to fuck you here with my fingers, the next time I taste you," he said, his voice low and gravelly.

"Is that a promise?"

He pressed his thumb just inside me, and I gasped at the foreign pleasure of it. "Yes."

"I need you," I panted, pushing my ass closer to him. "Don't make me wait."

His chest vibrated with his growl, and he thrust inside me a moment later, his finger still in my ass.

The sensation was too much, and I shattered with another cry, my hips jerking and my body tightening around his erection.

As I came down from the climax, Rhett gritted out, "The way you use my cock drives me fucking insane."

"Then stop holding back."

He snarled, abandoning my asshole to grip my backside with both hands.

He slammed into me, and I made a sound I wasn't sure I ever had before.

My cries grew more frantic as our bodies moved together, thrusting and rocking.

When I finally lost control again, we came together.

I collapsed on the bed on my face as the final waves of pleasure rolled through me. I was still dizzy, and tired, and hungry—but none of those things mattered.

I was too blissed-out to care.

"Survival would've been a lot more fun if we could fuck through it," I mumbled. "You should suggest that to Christina.

Rhett laughed, the sound free and happy in a way I didn't think I'd ever heard him. It made my lips curve upward against the mattress. "You can suggest it yourself when you meet her."

"Do I have to?"

"Yes. Everyone will give us a week or two to adjust to the bond, and then they'll start bugging us. They'll want us to take over my parents' old place in the Society's leadership."

I sat up quickly, sliding off Rhett's cock as I did. "They'll *what*?"

The motion was too much.

My world spun violently, and I had to grab his arm to stop myself from falling over.

He grabbed me, pulling me into his arms as he swore. "I should've fed you."

"I don't want food," I mumbled back. It was a lie. I wanted food. It just wasn't my first priority after the bomb he'd dropped on me. "Tell me about the Society."

"I'll tell you whatever you want to know when you're not about to pass out in my arms, Chaos."

He pulled me close and carried me out of the bedroom all while my world kept spinning.

Maybe that was a good call.

twenty

ERIN

RHETT SET me on the countertop, ignoring the fact that our releases had literally drenched me between my thighs. The feeling wasn't a pleasant one, but I was too dizzy to move.

As he stormed to the fridge, he growled out, "I will tie you to a fucking chair if you try to get down, Chaos. Don't test me."

The command alone made me itch to do exactly that.

And being tied to a chair sounded kind of hot.

I doubted he'd actually go through with it, but the allure was real.

When he opened the fridge, I saw that it was packed with premade meals we just needed to throw in the oven or heat up. Rhett stuck a massive pan of pasta in the oven, then grabbed a loaf of french bread off a mountain of baked goods.

Before he pulled it out of the bag, he looked back at the pile.

The bread was abandoned a moment later, and he carried a huge box of pastries over to me. I stared down at the sugary treats after he opened it up.

"What are your favorites?" he asked. The growl in his voice told me he wasn't going to take no for an answer, even though sugar didn't sound appealing to me in the slightest.

"Croissants, and donuts rolled in sugar." I pointed to the sugar-covered donut in the corner. "Unless there's filling in it. I think filling donuts with anything should be a crime."

Rhett's lips twitched, but he glanced back at the pile of baked goods and studied it for a moment.

Then he closed the box of pastries, walked away for a moment, and came back with a box of croissants.

They were all different, infused with a variety of things. I grabbed one that looked like it had pesto in it, and groaned when I took a bite.

Delicious.

My stomach rumbled loudly, as if it had been woken up by the glorious bite.

I held it out to Rhett. "You have to try this."

His attention was on my face. "You want it. It's yours."

I scowled. "I'm not eating more unless you're sharing. You need way more food to survive than I do."

Rhett's chest rumbled unhappily, but he finally caught my wrist and guided the croissant to his mouth. When he took a bite, his eyes closed. "Damn."

"I've had more to eat than you over the last month. You might be good at ignoring it, but you probably need to recover as much as I do." I took another bite of the bread, then made him polish off the last of it. "I need to use the bathroom."

"No. Get off the countertop, and I tie you to the chair." He picked up another croissant and held it up for me to take a bite. There was a light citrus smell coming off it that made me think it was orange flavored.

Sure enough, the combination of flaky, layered pastry and orange glaze made me moan.

"Keep that up, and I'm going to end up fucking you on this countertop," Rhett warned.

When I looked down, I saw him hardening.

"You can't be ready to go again yet. I don't think that's even physically possible."

"I'm a fae male with a compatible mate whose pheromones are singing for me, Chaos. It's possible." He stepped closer.

My legs wrapped around his waist of their own volition, but he didn't do anything about it.

"You need to eat more." He lifted the croissant back to my lips, and I dutifully took another bite.

By the time the spaghetti was warm, we'd demolished the entire box of croissants. I already felt sick, but one look at Rhett told me he wasn't going to let me go until I ate some pasta too.

So, when he set the huge casserole dish full of spaghetti and meatballs beside me, I ate some slowly, just to appease him.

The pleasure in his eyes while he ate with me told me that Kyle's nickname for him wasn't just a joke. Rhett really did love pasta.

And that made me smile.

When we were done, I was so full I couldn't keep my eyes open. Rhett carried me back to the bed, and I curled up against him, falling asleep almost instantly.

THE SUN WAS SHINING BRIGHTLY through the large windows in our room when I finally woke up. Groaning, I pressed my eyes against his skin.

As expected, my entire body was draped over Rhett's.

His hands were on my ass, but his grip was relaxed and his chest rose and fell steadily.

He was still sleeping.

His erection was pressed against my core, and apparently had been for a long time, considering I was crazy slick with desire. I didn't dare let myself move while he was sleeping. We hadn't talked about whether or not we were okay with that, and I wasn't about to risk making him uncomfortable.

Even though I was horny as hell and desperate to let myself move like I wanted to. It wouldn't take much effort to get myself off.

I waited as long as I could, but the slickness grew worse, and my desire grew fiercer.

When I couldn't wait any longer, I finally eased myself off his body.

By some miracle, he didn't wake up.

My legs shook as I padded into the bathroom, quietly closing the door before I turned the shower on.

Quiet orgasms weren't really a talent of mine, but it would work as white noise.

I didn't bother getting in the shower, just sat down on the ledge of the tub and parted my thighs. My head tipped back at the first brush of my fingers to my clit, and I bit the inside of my cheek to stop myself from moaning.

I circled it again, and again.

My legs parted wider.

My breathing grew ragged.

I was close.

So, so close.

I—

A cry escaped me as a large hand closed around my wrist,

moving it away from my core just before a thick, hot tongue dragged over my clit.

My hips jerked as I nearly came, but he pulled away before I could get off.

My body was tense with need, my chest rising and falling rapidly, as I opened my eyes and found myself staring down at a gorgeous, furious male fae.

"What are you doing, Chaos?"

"Seems pretty obvious. I needed to get off." My chest rose and fell rapidly.

"If you needed to get off, you would've told me. That's my job. Instead, you turned the shower on so I wouldn't hear you. You snuck out of my bed. You started pleasuring *yourself*."

"I almost finished, too," I gritted out.

"You hid from me." His words were a low growl. "Have you been faking your orgasms? I—"

"You were sleeping," I interrupted him. "I would never fake an orgasm. I wanted to let you sleep, and I was horny. That's all there is to it, okay? You could've gotten me off twice in the amount of time I've spent in here, so obviously you're not lacking anything. I was just trying to be nice."

The anger in his gaze eased. "Sleep doesn't matter to me. You do. If you're horny, wake me up."

"Okay." I bit my lip, still breathing hard. My core was starting to ache. "I kind of panicked. I woke up with your cock between my thighs, and I was slick with need, and I wanted you badly. But I didn't want to just use you, or make you feel violated, or—"

"Do you know the words that seal the bond, Erin?"

His use of my name caught me off guard. I shook my head.

"I'm yours," he said. "It's as simple as that. *I'm yours.* So if you want to ride me while I'm sleeping, ride me. Waking up with you wrapped around my cock, getting yourself off, would be a fucking dream."

My thighs clenched. "Are you going to do the same if you wake up horny?"

"Only if you want me to."

I let myself imagine being woken up by his tongue on my clit. His hand between my thighs. His cock filling me.

My breathing picked up again. "I want you to."

Rhett's chest rumbled.

He opened my thighs wider, leaning in to lick me again. One of his hands found my back entrance, the other on my thigh, as he ate me out.

This time, he didn't pull away until I was crying out with pleasure.

Afterward, he bent me over the edge of the tub and fucked me until we came together.

Throughout all of it, two words ran through my mind as if on repeat.

I'm yours.

I'm yours.

I'm yours.

WE SPENT THE DAY EATING, lounging, and screwing.

It was blissful.

Every time we were together, I got closer to saying the words out loud.

I'm yours.

But I didn't say them.

We fell asleep on the couch that night, an action movie playing while we drifted off. I was safe, happy, and content in a way I hoped would never end.

And there was a way to ensure it never could.

One I started to actually *want* as time continued to go by.

THE SUN DIDN'T WAKE me up the next morning.

It wasn't even rising yet as I opened my eyes, heat coursing through my veins and pushing me to get up.

Rhett's cock was wedged between my ass cheeks, my back was to his chest, and his fingers were between my thighs. All I had on was a pair of his sweats that had been rolled up a few times at my waist before he pushed them down in my sleep. He touched my tits too much to bother with a shirt. It would've just annoyed us both.

My hips arched my ass against his cock as he made a slow circle around my clit. His fingers were drenched with my desire—and probably some of his release from the night before.

I sucked in a breath as one of his fingers slowly slid inside me. It didn't have anything on his cock, but still felt good.

"Couldn't sleep?" I murmured, rocking my hips.

"Dreamed of you." He lifted my thigh over his, opening me up wider as he shifted positions, lining his cock up with my slit. "I need you, Chaos."

The words made me ache in the very best way.

He needed me.

He wanted me.

He cared about me.

I moved my hips, taking the tip of him, and he groaned as he thrust upward.

He felt amazing—but after all the sex we'd been having, I wanted more.

"Shift," I breathed.

He growled. "I barely have control right now, Chaos. Don't push me."

Thrill had my back arching, and he snarled at the way it pressed him against my inner walls.

"Shift, Rhetti," I commanded.

Instead of giving me what I wanted, he lifted me off his cock.

I glowered at him as he turned me around in his arms—but the glare vanished as he sat up and set me back down, facing him.

And as he pulled me down, seating me on his erection.

His eyes were hot, but slightly vulnerable. "I dreamed you were leaving me. Throwing a ring at me."

"I don't have a ring to throw."

His grip on my hips tightened. "I'm buying you a ring, Erin. This is real. You're going to be my wife as much as you're my mate."

My body clenched around his cock, but he didn't budge.

I put my hands on his face. "I chose you, Rhett. I want you. I'm not throwing the ring, and I'm not leaving. You're stuck with me."

He kissed me hard.

Rough.

Burying his hands in my hair, he tilted my head back, opening me up as his tongue worked mine.

I gasped against his mouth as his cock swelled inside me, so thick I wasn't sure I could move on it at all. I was soaked, but he was—

"Shit," I choked out, opening my eyes as his wings spread out behind him. They were pressed against the couch, but the intensity in his eyes said he didn't care.

I lifted a hand to one of the horns on his head, and he gritted his teeth, throbbing hard inside me.

I needed more.

I needed *him*.

Permanently.

I wasn't going to let him fade. I needed him, and wanted him, and hell, maybe even loved him. I couldn't let him go.

So I finally let the words out. "I'm yours, Rhetti."

His eyes burned me. "Are you sure?"

I reached for his wing with my free hand, trailing it toward the outside, where he'd never let me touch because it was too sensitive.

He gritted his jaw, his gaze flooded with the need he was fighting.

"Positive. I'm yours, whether you want me or—"

"I want you. I always want you. I'm yours, Chaos."

He thrust into me, and a scream of pleasure tore through my lungs as fire raced through my veins and down my spine.

We came together, and a foreign weight settled on my shoulders. I leaned against his chest, panting as I wrapped my arms around his neck to hold myself up.

"I have wings now?"

"You do. They match mine."

So they were the same as the gorgeous, colorless appendages on his back.

Something inside me settled at the clear evidence that he belonged to me and I belonged to him. I hadn't seen them, but they were a marking that no one could erase.

He tipped my head back, lowering his lips to mine and kissing me lightly.

Slowly.

Deeply.

I kissed him back, until his fingertips brushed the top curve of one of my wings. The touch was so light, I should've barely felt it, but the sensation was insane.

My hips jerked violently, my teeth cutting into Rhett's lip as the orgasm tore through me like electricity.

"Sorry—I'm sorry, I—Rhett!" My shriek accompanied another arch of my hips, my body way too responsive to the pressure against my wing.

When I lifted my head, sucking in deep breaths as I tried to recover, I found him grinning wickedly.

He'd done that on purpose.

"I'm going to kill you." There was no bite behind the words. They actually came out a little breathy.

"Do you really want to kill me, Chaos?" One of his hands found my breast, his thumb dragging slowly over my nipple. "Or do you just want me to fuck you harder?"

I groaned.

My body tightened around his cock.

"That's what I thought." He lifted me off his erection, and set me down on my stomach on the ottoman. My hands spread over the cushions, and he opened my legs wide before thrusting into me again.

All my thoughts died as he dragged orgasm after orgasm out of me until I was so well-pleasured, I could barely move.

Sealing the mate bond was a good thing.

A very, very good thing.

I was never letting go of Rhett.

RHETT

"SO, you think they're going to pick us to lead the Society with Cameron and Molly," Erin said, lifting a spoonful of chili to her lips.

The same lips that had been wrapped around my cock twenty minutes ago.

Fuck, I was getting hard again already.

We'd gone flying earlier, and it had been a blast. The flying had been followed by sex. So fucking much sex.

Our need would ease when her pheromones faded, but until then, I would enjoy every minute of it. We were already a week into the bond, so it was easing up slightly for her, at least.

I didn't think it would ever ease up for me.

"They will," I agreed. "We'll get voted into the second or third position. The vote is still a few months out, though."

"Who else will get chosen?"

I shrugged. "No one else has the connections Cam and I have, so it's hard to say."

Erin nodded slowly. "I can't say it's what I wanted to do, but I guess it's better than sitting around and doing nothing. Or being rejected for promotions because there are humans who want it."

"They shouldn't have done that to you."

"It's fine. It got me to you, which is what matters, right?"

"Yes." I put my hand on her thigh, squeezing.

"What do we do until then?" she asked. "You can't guard for the game shows anymore, unless you leave me."

The hesitation in her eyes told me she thought that was an actual option.

"That's not happening," I said bluntly. "You're mine, remember? I'm not walking away."

Her hesitation disappeared.

Her shoulders lifted a little higher.

"I promised I'd find Kyle's sister a mate," I said with a grimace. "She's... difficult."

"More difficult than me?" Erin lifted an eyebrow.

"She's had hundreds of years to perfect hers, so yes. And you're not difficult; you're stubborn."

"Stubborn is just another way to say *independent and confident*. Difficult is too."

I chuckled. "Usually, I would agree with you, but Kenna is a different kind of difficult. The kind that occurs when you're one of very, very few fae women, and both spoiled and adored by everyone you meet."

"Oh." Erin's forehead creased. "Then why isn't she mated yet? Isn't Kyle pretty old?"

"She's about fifty years younger than him, so she has about fifty years left. Most male fae have heard stories about her, and avoid her because of them. She had men chasing her before the war, but now that there are compatible humans..."

"Ah. Well, you know someone who could make her happy?"

"I know a few guys who haven't met her, who could probably get along with her," I agreed. "While Kyle's on the island, it'll be much easier to pair her off. He's protective."

"I did get that vibe from him." Erin took another bite.

Damn, those lips...

She said, "So, we'll spend the next few months finding Kenna a mate. But there are still a lot of things we haven't talked about. Like kids. I'm on birth control now, and don't intend to get off it anytime soon." She eyed me, like she was waiting for me to protest.

"It's very difficult for fae to have kids. It usually takes a century or more for a couple to get pregnant. Even in the days when I wanted to take a mate, I never planned or expected children. If you decide you want to try, then we'll try, and see what happens. If not, we won't."

"I can get behind that plan." She took another bite. "What about hobbies? You haven't mentioned anything about those."

"My only hobby has been work." I lifted a shoulder. "I watch movies when I need to decompress, if that counts."

"It does." She nodded approval.

"What about you?"

"I like to keep busy, and my job wasn't where it's at, so I've tried a lot of things. My favorites are cooking and this Pilates class I used to take."

"Pilates?" I raised an eyebrow.

"I know it doesn't sound fun, but it is."

"We'll sign up for a class here, then."

"We?" She lifted her eyebrows at me. "*You're* going to do Pilates?"

"Sure."

Her lips split in a grin. "I'm holding you to that, even if you get embarrassed."

"I don't get embarrassed. Even if it's ridiculous, I'll get to watch your body move as we do it." I reached over and pinched her nipple lightly through one of my t-shirts with a cutout for the wings. It was far too big for her, so I could see her entire ass through it when she walked around. It was fucking gorgeous.

"You do know what it is," she tossed back.

"I've never done it, though."

"That's acceptable. You'll be disappointed by how well my sports bras do their job, though."

"A month on an island forced me to get used to that."

She laughed. "I guess it did."

We were halfway through eating when there was a knock at our door.

I looked at Erin.

She looked at me. "Any idea who it is?"

"No, but I'll answer it. You need to eat."

I crossed the house with my mate close at my heels. I shouldn't have expected her to stay at the table. When she was interested in something, her determination was unmatched.

All she had on was one of my shirts, so I tucked her against my side as I pulled the door open.

When I found Cameron, Molly, Christina, and Charlie on our porch, I blinked.

It had only been a week.

"We couldn't wait any longer to meet you and congratulate you! You guys were adorable on the show!" Molly exclaimed, stepping into the house and throwing her arms around Erin without touching her wings. Erin's gaze jerked to me, a little panicked about the sudden physical contact.

I shrugged. I hadn't seen much of Molly being her genuine self, given how she and Cam had been playing the game when they were on the island.

"Also, Christina got us the first episode of the third season," she added. "Keep it on the down-low, because it's kind of an abuse of power."

"It's not an abuse," Christina protested, stepping into the house. She gave me a quick hug, then engulfed Erin, who was finally free from Molly. "It's an *advantage*. There has to be *some* advantage to the thankless work we do."

"Well, this advantage is worth it. I'm dying to see who wins the next season. Kyle has to pull it out one of these times," Molly said. "We're waiting to watch it with you guys. Christina made dinner, if you're up for joining us at their place?" She looked at Erin with what could only be hope.

Erin looked at me again.

I gave her a small smile. It was her call. I didn't mind either way.

"Sounds like fun," Erin finally said, her voice more confident than she really was. "Give me a few minutes to put on some pants, and we'll head over."

Molly smiled widely, and hugged Erin again.

Erin was more prepared for it that time, and hugged her back more than she had before.

"Awesome! Welcome to the family!" Molly exclaimed.

We closed the door as they all headed to Charlie and Christina's place a few houses down, and Erin looked at me.

"We don't have to go," I told her. "I can tell them I'm not in the mood."

"I know. But I kind of want to," she admitted. "It could be nice to have a family. And we *have* to watch, considering what Kyle and Chris did for us."

"Then let's find your pants. And a bra."

We'd have to tie the shirt beneath her wings, but we'd done it earlier when we went flying, so I knew she wouldn't mind.

I captured her hand as we made our way to the bedroom.

"Do you think they'll like me?" she asked, as she pulled the waistband of her leggings into place.

"They'd be stupid not to." I pulled her into my arms and kissed her, slowly. "But it doesn't matter whether they do, because I love you, Chaos. And that will never change."

Her eyes flooded with tears, and she pulled my face down to hers, kissing me hard before she released me. "I love you too, Rhetti Spaghetti."

I snorted, and she laughed.

Tugging her harder to my chest, I kissed her deeply until she pushed me away.

Breathlessly, she said, "We've got a family to win over. Let's go."

My lips curved upward as we walked out together.

I'd been a moron for thinking I didn't want to find love.

epilogue

"I CAN'T BELIEVE we're planning a wedding for this crazy fae chick," I grumbled to Rhett, looking up from my laptop and the folder of information we'd been putting together. He was working on the same thing, with his own laptop open as we sat together at our kitchen table. "*We* didn't even have a wedding, and I used to be human."

He looked up from his computer. "We can have a wedding if you want."

Though I wouldn't give up the sparkly ring he'd bought me over my dead body, I wrinkled my nose at the idea of a wedding. "Pass. I just want to be done with this diva."

We had spent *months* trying to find the woman a mate. As much as we'd needed Kyle on Survival, we'd definitely gotten the worse end of the bargain. Rhett had been being nice when he said the woman was difficult. I wanted to strangle her every time we saw her.

Sure, she was smart and strong, but I was of the opinion we should throw her on Survival just to humble her a little.

Considering she was already a fae woman, it would never happen.

But damn, a girl could dream.

I kept hoping Kyle would win *Survival* and take over the wedding plans. We'd convinced her to pick a guy, and they were head-over-heels for each other, but she was still being a diva about everything. And because she wouldn't seal the bond until it was *perfect*, we were stuck dealing with her out of obligation to the bastard.

The fifth season was nearly over, and Kyle clearly wasn't going to win it. Though he got to the end every time, he'd made a habit of helping pair the human women off with the perfect guy, then helping that guy get to the end.

He'd gotten Julian and Harker mated since we left the island. Chris was well on his way there, too.

But the bastard looked skinnier and more tired with every season.

His energy was running low.

Rhett was pretty sure he was running out of time.

Christina claimed she had an ace in her pocket to get Kyle paired off, but I wasn't sure that even she could manage that. He had learned a lot about women since his first season, but he was still a pain in the ass.

Kind of like his sister.

I heard a thunderclap outside, and looked out the large windows that gave us a view of the ocean in our backyard.

Damn, it was gorgeous.

"Remember that first night I basically forced you to snuggle with me?" I asked him, staring at the rain with something that felt surprisingly like fondness.

Maybe even a little bit of yearning.

Those had been rough, shitty days, but I'd come to cherish the memories. The ones that included snuggling with Rhett, at least.

"I wanted to sit you on my lap and wrap you in my wings so you would stop shivering," he admitted, looking at the rain too.

A sudden urge overwhelmed me, and I stood. My chair scratched the tile as I moved it, but I ignored the cringe-worthy sound.

Rhett's amused expression told me he knew I'd had some sort of idea.

When I grabbed his hand, he abandoned his laptop without question and let me tow him outside.

"What are we doing now, Chaos?"

"You'll see," I promised.

More thunder rumbled in the sky, and we stepped off the porch, into the rain.

I closed my eyes as it fell on my head and down my face, tipping my head back so the water could roll over my skin.

Taking a deep breath in, I inhaled the familiar smell of a storm.

I'd hated the rain on the island, but it had given me everything I needed.

Rhett.

A family.

Happiness.

"Run with me!" I called to Rhett, lifting my face so I could meet his gaze.

"Run in the rain? I thought we're supposed to dance?" There was a teasing smile on his face.

His smiles had gotten bigger since we mated.

They lasted longer, too.

I had done that.

I hadn't hurt him, like I'd been worried about all those months ago. I'd healed him. Or helped him heal himself, at least.

The right kind of love could do that for a person, in the right situation.

"Then dance with me Rhetti."

He didn't wait for another order, dragging me into my arms before spinning me around in the sand. We were shitty dancers, stumbling more than we remained steady, but we laughed so hard that my lungs burned by the time we collapsed on the sand together.

I owed *Survival* everything.

Or maybe I owed the rain.

Either way, life was fucking beautiful.

Whew, this book took a lot of mental energy.
There were a lot of factors to juggle in this baby, and for whatever reason, book two is pretty much always harder to write than book one. It was also a little more serious, with a little more suffering in the rain, and I hate writing about suffering. I love the light, fluffy stuff, and the puns.
Puns are life.
But here we are. We made it, wooooo! And I absolutely *loved* Rhett and Erin's story!
As you may have guessed, Kyle's will be the third (and last) book in this series. I'm really excited to see how things work out between him and his lady!
Anyway, I hope you loved Rhett and Erin as much as I did.
And I hope you check out Kyle's book, *Heat & Hard Candies*!
Until next time,
All the love,
Lola Glass <3

stay in touch

If you want to receive Lola's newsletter for new releases (no spam!) use this link:

<u>LINK</u>

Or find her on:
FACEBOOK
TIKTOK
INSTAGRAM
PINTEREST
GOODREADS

all series by lola glass

Standalones:

Survival of the Mated

Mate Mountain

Wildwood

Deceit & Devotion

Claimed by the Wolf

Forbidden Mates

Wild Hunt

Kings of Disaster

Night's Curse

Outcast Pack

Feral Pack

Mate Hunt

Series:

Burning Kingdom

Sacrificed to the Fae King

Shifter Queen

Wolfsbane

Shifter City

Supernatural Underworld

Moon of the Monsters

Rejected Mate Refuge

Lola is a book-lover with a *slight* romance obsession and a passion for love—real love. Not the flowers-and-chocolates kind of love, but the kind where two people build a relationship strong enough to last. That's the kind of relationship she loves to read about, and the kind she tries to portray in her books.

Even though they're fun stories about sassy women and huge, growly magical men ;)